My Own Worst Nightmare

By Heather McGhee

WorldMaker Media
www.worldmakermedia.com

To my husband for his patience, his impatience and his ability to make me laugh, whether I want to or not.

WorldMaker Media
P.O. Box 610383
Newton, MA 02461
www.worldmakermedia.com

Cover Design by Amy Rooney

Chapter One

"Did you hear what your father did last week?" Michael asked as I came into the portable office building one hot August afternoon, wiping sweat and sawdust off my brow.

"Hear about what?" I went straight to the cooler, downing two cups of cool water to soothe my scratchy, dust-coated throat. The day was too damn hot and sticky to be building houses, but someone had to do it.

"Mr. Watson sold the company."

I sputtered, dripping water down my grimy t-shirt. "He did *what?*"

Michael shrugged, "He sold the company."

I unbuckled my tool belt, dropped it on a nearby table, and marched across the small, narrow room to my father's office, not bothering to knock. "What's this about you selling the company?"

Henry Watson looked up from his computer and muttered, "I'm going to fire Michael for sure this time. Damn fool can't keep his mouth shut."

"Never mind Michael. You sold the company? Why didn't you tell me?"

"I was made an offer I couldn't refuse," he said, looking at me, his twenty-nine-year-old tomboy of a daughter, as though I was a lost cause. "I haven't made my retirement a secret. It's past time I rested these weary bones, and your mother wants to travel. I've put this off long enough."

"Oh, Daddy," I groaned, slumping into a chair. "Is

1

this why you were in Dallas all last week? I thought you were visiting Aunt Gracie."

"I did see Gracie, *and* I sold the company."

I stared at him. He was deliberately being obtuse with me. I could always tell. I did the same thing to him all the time. It was all part of that wonderful father-daughter bond of ours. "You didn't tell me. You told Michael, your gopher, but you didn't tell me. I'm insulted."

"Actually, everyone knew," he replied in a vague way. I shot out of my chair.

"*What?*"

Daddy slanted me a look "If I had told you, you would have done something foolish to stop the sale. I couldn't have that."

"So, you just kept it a secret from me?" I crossed my arms over my chest and pouted. I wasn't *that* bad. I might have understood...maybe. "If you really wanted to sell that badly, why didn't you offer it to me? I would have bought it."

He shook his head and leaned back in his chair. "You can't afford it, and you know it. This company has been in the red for two years now. The construction business is not what it used to be."

"Yeah, but..."

"No buts," he sternly admonished. "I wasn't just thinking of your mother when I decided this. You can't slave away here forever. It's time you set up your own business. Do something with that degree I paid for."

I crinkled my brow. "What are you talking about? I have a degree in architectural design. I'm using that degree. Why the hell do you think I've worked here for the past five years?"

"Constructing bearing walls and lugging around insulation is not using your degree," he countered.

"I help out where I can," I said meekly. "Besides, those houses out there are my designs. So there, I do use my degree."

"Those house designs were drawn up four years ago. You haven't done anything new since then. And I understand that. They are great designs and the reason we even secured the financing for this development. But look at you, Lily, you're a mess. I never see you in anything besides ratty jeans, your hair's been in that ponytail for the past year, and your hands – good Lord – you have enough calluses to use them for a sanding block."

I opened my palms, seeing the rough skin and grimaced. My last manicure was...well, too long for me to even remember. Daddy kept talking, leaving behind the original subject. But the next topic of discussion was one never far away in his mind.

"How am I supposed to have any grandchildren if the only time a man can stand to be near you is when you're hanging wallboard together?" That came out as a joke, but the truth still hurt every time him and Momma pointed it out to me.

"You have a grandchild," I mumbled, crossing my arms again and staring down at the floor. My biological clock didn't tick all that often yet, but Momma and Daddy were determined to keep it wound up for me and primed for a resounding alarm.

"Step-grandchild," he corrected. "Brianna is a joy to spoil, but it's not the same. We missed all the baby clothes and diaper changing, and late night feeding."

"Oh, yeah, that sounds grand."

Daddy eyed me over the expanse of his desk. "You should feel fortunate to not be in your sister's shoes. It breaks my heart to know Marissa can't have children."

I huffed out a heavy breath. "Don't tell Bri that. She'll never let you live it down."

"As long as you keep your trap shut, she won't know, now will she?"

I averted my gaze, not wanting to talk about my non-existent love life, my empty womb, or the pains of my sister. If I ever felt the desire for that kind of torture, I only had to wait a few days. The subject would come up again. It always did.

For five years, I labored in Daddy's construction business, but ever since I could walk, I played among the skeletal structures of new buildings and in the large dirt mounds and sand hills, constructing my own doll homes and play forts from the scrap lumber. Sawdust and tile grout ran through my veins. I just couldn't believe that he'd sell the company. All that I knew would soon be taken away from me.

After my ugly divorce, working for Daddy had been my security blanket. I didn't have to worry about striking out on my own because I always had a place here. I loved every part of my job, and I'd be the first to admit that I hid behind it. In a way, I never grew up. College, my marriage, buying my own home – those were just steps to becoming an adult. But that didn't mean much. I'm just as hard-headed and impatient as a ten-year-old child. It seemed that my time for maturity was upon me now.

And I didn't like it one bit.

"So who do I work for now?"

"Bryce King," he answered. "But you don't work for him. I've seen to that."

I ignored that last part. "Bryce King? The billionaire from Texas? He'll ruin us!"

"Millionaire," Daddy corrected me again. "And no, he won't. He's the CEO of one of the top financial restoration companies in the region."

"He's a shark! He buys companies and takes them apart for the fun of it."

"Mr. King saves companies like this one. You should meet him before you start putting him into categories. He's a nice man with humble beginnings. He will be good for Watson Construction."

I faced the tiny window. "But all those people out there, Daddy! What if this Mr. King decides to close us down? They won't have a job anymore."

"I've seen to that, too," he said.

"How?"

"An agreement...a stipulation on the sale, if you will. Mr. King won't change anything concerning the employees' contracts for the next year. By then, if the company is still in the red, he has the right to make cutbacks."

I watched the swarm of workers on the nearest house, a modern twist on a turn-of-the-century townhouse. Stout Agusto, lumbering up a makeshift incline with a load of joists on his shoulder; bony Mark and his brother Johnny, feeding plywood through a table saw; Bently, who always had a smile on his face, rolling a wheelbarrow of debris out to a dumpster. The names and faces of every man and woman who worked for Watson Construction flashed across my mind like frames on a movie real. Ginger, our main office receptionist with more gold in her heart than Fort Knox; Tony, the skittish and nerdy accountant; Michael, the misunderstood assistant; Delmar, the oldest carpenter alive; Miguel, Cory, Eddie, Joseph…

"And after a year? What happens then?" I turned back to my father, meeting his gaze solidly.

He sighed heavily. "If the company must be dissolved, then those with contracts will be given a leave settlement comprisable to six months pay and dismissed."

I studied him. This can't be happening. Those people were friends. His friends! "How much?"

"What?" He leaned forward to catch my quiet question.

"How much were you offered?"

"Enough."

"Enough for what?" My voice rose, but I didn't care. Daddy darted a glance to his door, which I had left open, and into the rest of the portable where Michael was still shuffling around at his desk. I was sure he heard every word up to this point. I closed the door and repeated, "Enough for what?"

"Enough to settle our debts and set aside some money for you and your sister."

That struck me, and I reared back, amazed. "What about you? How much are you getting out of this?"

"Nothing," he said, peering at me oddly. "My retirement and military pension have been covering my expenses for years now. I haven't pulled a paycheck from this company in twenty-two months. The money from the sale is yours and Marissa's."

I blinked a few times. "You haven't collected a check in two years? You never said anything."

"It wasn't important. Besides, your mother and I have decided to sell the house, and buy a vacation home on the coast," he answered my question and my thoughts.

"What?! You're leaving, too? Why don't you ever tell me these things? Does Marissa know?"

"It's never been a secret, Lil Lil. Nomi has wanted to return home for years now. So, we're moving back to Pebble Beach." His brow smoothed over quickly, but I didn't miss the tiny frown line that popped up.

"You hate Pebble Beach," I reminded him.

He smiled, resembling a love-struck teenager. "But I love your mother, and I would follow those legs of hers across the globe."

I returned to my chair, grumbling under my breath. This had started out as a good day. Although it was only Tuesday, the temperature had dropped a few degrees since yesterday, and no one had complained about anything so far – no "the electrician is late again," no "I need to leave early today," and no fights between Mark and Johnny for sure.

"Speaking of love," he started again. I jerked my

eyes to him. *Oh, God, not again…he lasted fifteen minutes this time.* "When am I going to get my grandchildren?"

I grinned maliciously. "If you're in such a hurry, I can drag Bently off behind the Porta-Potty, and get knocked up today."

"Bently?" he asked as his eyebrows hit the ceiling. "You and Bently?"

Groaning and rolling my eyes, I said, "No, Daddy. I was joking. Bently's married, remember? To my best friend, Ann. I was the maid of honor."

"Oh, right," he cleared his throat. "Is there, uh…anyone else you've been dragging behind the Porta-Potty? I think Michael might have a thing for you."

Dearest Daddy, I thought. *He doesn't have a clue.* Michael wouldn't be caught behind a Porta-Potty with any woman – Eddie, maybe, but not a woman. "I think Michael has other plans for his life," I said calmly.

Just then, poor Michael knocked on the door and poked his head in. "Lily, you're wanted on site four. Something about the measurements in the master bath not adding up, and they can't fit the Jacuzzi through."

"We'll talk about this later," I told Daddy and headed out into the August sunshine to do my job.

~~~~~

Bryce King sat behind his desk two days later and stared at the woman in front of him. "You are sincere about this?"

"Absolutely," Kristen said firmly, nodding her

perfectly made-up head, not a hair shaking loose. "I've had enough of your lies."

"I have never lied to you, Kristen. I informed you beforehand. It was a business dinner," he said for what seemed like the hundredth time. She lifted a tanned shoulder, not believing him.

"Vivian Corter does not do business. She is out to get you for herself, and I will not stand by waiting for that to happen. I am leaving while I still have my dignity."

Bryce clenched his fists under the desk, taking a deep breath and speaking through his teeth, "Ms. Corter solicited my opinion about a business prospect. You are making a mountain out of a molehill."

An icy glare followed. "Do not speak to me that way. You are not a boy from the streets anymore. Do not insult the man you have become."

"And what kind of man am I, Kris?"

She looked away, staring out the massive windows that overlooked all of downtown Dallas. "You are a shrewd, handsome, wealthy businessman, Bryce, but you are still too naïve for your own good." She met his gaze again. "Every person in this city knows Vivian's capacity for getting what she wants. You do not wish to see that, but it is only a matter of time before you fall for her schemes. I have not been, nor will I ever be, second in line to any woman."

He unclenched his jaw to speak, but was interrupted by his secretary. "Mr. King," Gloria said through the phone's intercom, "Justin is here to see you."

Bryce punched a button. "Give me a few minutes,

Gloria." But Kristen was already standing and shouldering her leather handbag. "This isn't over between us, Kris."

A sad gloom filled her eyes. "Yes, Bryce, I am afraid it is definitely over." Then she turned and walked out of his life. He should have felt troubled by her leaving, but something akin to relief settled under his skin instead. Kristen had always been too narcissistic for him. And now that she was gone, he couldn't remember why they had been together for so long. Great sex, maybe?

Gloria popped her head in a few seconds later. "You okay, Mr. King?"

He glanced at her. "I'm fine. Send in Justin."

His business associate, Justin Marshal, came swiftly through the door. Justin did everything swiftly - walking, eating, talking, waiting in line at the DMV. He also had this astute mind that remembered the oddest tidbits of information, like the fact that a flamingo can only eat with its head upside down. Justin tossed a file on Bryce's desk. "Have a look at this."

Bryce pushed Kris out of his thoughts and opened the file. "What am I looking at?"

Justin hurried around the side of the desk and hovered over his shoulder. "This is from that construction company you bought. The one in Arkansas?"

"Watson Construction," Bryce said, flipping through the papers.

"Yeah, that one. This is what I wanted to show you." He pushed the top sheets aside and thumped his finger on a miniature house plan. "Look familiar?"

Bryce studied the plan. "No, should it?"

"Remember that architecture firm outside of Grand Prairie that you wanted, but the owner wouldn't sell?"

"Yeah."

"These are the same houses." Justin folded his arms across his chest, staring down at the plans.

"Sorry, Justin. Kris has managed to stupefy me once today. Explain the problem," Bryce said, looking closer. If he remembered correctly, the reason he even wanted that firm was because his baby sister had fallen in love with a house and wanted to build one on her own property. He traced the home plans back to a small design firm, but before Bryce could exert enough pressure on the owner, the firm closed shop. The architect's name was...Nicolas something.

"Look at the designer," Justin pointed out. Bryce scanned the page. Lily Watson.

"That can't be right."

"It is," Justin claimed. "I looked it all up." He shoved the plans aside to the last page. A detailed track sheet of Lily Watson's career covered the entire page. Graduate of Kansas State, with a masters in architectural design and a minor in software development; intern to Jenson's Designs out of Kansas City; site manager to Watson Construction. A post-it note stuck to the bottom: *Nicolas Garcia, also graduated from K-State, same year.*

"This Lily Watson stole someone's design?"

Justin shook his head. "I don't know. But if that is true, we've got problems. We've closed the deal on the

Watson Company, but if it's involved in fraud, we'll need to do some serious damage control. And we absolutely don't want Morrissey getting wind of this."

This day just gets better and better, Bryce thought. *And it's only Thursday. The crazy stuff doesn't start until Saturday.* "How many of these houses has Watson built?"

"None completed so far. They are working on a new development. Some kind of miniature, man-made lake community. All the houses use these plans, which incorporate some kind of architectural software. There will be fourteen houses when they're done building, but all of them are accounted for. We'll have a severe law suit if fourteen families don't get the homes they paid for."

He buzzed Gloria into his office. "Get me a flight to Little Rock as soon as you can." Then he turned to Justin, "Find that Nicolas guy from Grand Prairie. Figure out what's going on here. Discreetly. And then get a hold of our attorneys. Ask them to go through the contracts again. Then warn Jacobson about preparing a statement for the press, just in case."

His associate rushed out of the room, brushing by Gloria so that she stumbled back a step. "Gracious, that man. Doesn't he ever slow down?"

"That's why I like him," Bryce smiled grimly at his secretary and then returned to the file. He looked up when he realized that she still stood in front of him. "Yes?"

"I was wondering if you need me to clear your afternoon, sir."

"Whatever for?"

She tilted her wire-rimmed glasses lower on her nose. "Because Miss Snob just dumped you, and you could use some time away from this place."

He opened his mouth to deny that fact, but closed it with a snap. Gloria had been his secretary since he was scrounging around in a dingy office building in Arlington, doing his best to pay the bills with a meager salary earned from advising small companies on ways to boost their business. She stuck with him through the rough times, and had earned the right to comment on his problems - especially since she wouldn't have listened to him anyway. Despite her ability to comment on any aspect of his life, she still called him "Mr. King."

"I think that would be a good idea. I need to go see Lisa anyway."

She nodded as though he had come to his senses and floated out of the room. An hour later, she confirmed his flight for the next morning, and he gathered his briefcase.

"Take the rest of the week off," he told her as he left. "And remind me to give you a raise when I get back."

She grinned. "You gave me one last week, Mr. King."

He halted at the outer door. "Oh, so I did. Well, you're due for another."

Chapter Two

His sister, Lisa, flung open the front door of her cedar-planked lake house with a giant smile on her face and a baby on her hip. "Bryce! You didn't tell me you were coming out today."

"I needed to get away from the city," he said, patting his nephew on the head and reaching over to give her a kiss on the cheek.

Lisa peered out into the yard before closing the door behind them. "Where's Kristen? She's usually with you."

"Kristen left me," he said, stepping over some toys in his dash to the kitchen and the closest, unopened beer bottle. He opened the refrigerator and pulled out an ice-cold brew, condensation spotting the dark glass as it met with warmer air, and sighed with satisfaction.

"Oh, no," Lisa cried, setting little Lenny in his high chair. "What happened?"

Before he could answer, the twins, Benji and Julian, galloped into the kitchen, screeching, "Uncle Bryce!" He put his beer on the counter and scooped each wiggly body in an arm, swinging them around.

"Good gracious! You two are getting heavy," he said, dropping them to the tiled floor. They landed in a pile, giggling and scampering to climb up his legs.

"They do tend to do that," his sister said, shooing her boys out the back door. "If you'd ever get married and have kids of your own – rather than borrowing mine – you'd know that."

Julian pushed Benji aside to reach the back deck first, and Benji shouted at him to "behave, or I'm not inviting you to my birthday party!" to which Julian replied, "It's my birthday, too, dummy!" As they galloped down the lawn to a haphazard tree fort, Bryce shuddered at the idea of being a father.

"Now, what happened to this one?" Lisa asked, rounding on him.

"Nothing," he shrugged, not really wanting to talk about Kris. He had left the city. He was twenty minutes away. He came out here to Lisa's corner of heaven to get away from the city and Kris and breathtaking views and copyrights...well, the copyrights, he came searching for, but that wasn't here nor there.

"Nothing? That's what you said about the last one. There has to be something. Were you rude to her?"

"No."

"Did you spend any time with her?"

"Yes."

"Were you cheating on her?"

He glared at his baby sister. "Why do you ask me the same questions every time I loose a girlfriend? Maybe she was cheating on me."

"Probably," Lisa agreed wholeheartedly. "But the women always leave you for some reason. That means it must be your fault. So, what did you do?"

"Absolutely nothing," he confirmed with a deep swig. "Kris left because she saw the future and didn't like it."

Lisa put her hands on her hips. "Oh well, I never liked her anyway."

Bryce choked on his beer through a laugh. "You never liked any of them."

"That's because they only want your money. Find a

woman that will tell you 'no' and I'll like that one."

"Kristen did tell me no," he said. "Today."

"Yeah, but only this one time. And if you really loved her, you wouldn't have let her go anyway."

"Don't start with the love thing again," he said, turning away from her as she reached into a cabinet for a box of cereal. "I'm not ready to settle down yet."

"You're thirty-six, Bryce," Lisa said. "When do you think you'll be ready to get married and have kids and all that? These boys are driving me crazy."

"Then have a girl," he retorted and immediately wished he'd kept his mouth shut. Lisa's sweet face contorted.

"*You* have a girl," she said back in a hurt voice.

"Lisa, I'm sorry. I didn't mean…"

She waved him off. "I know you didn't. And yes, I'd like to have a girl, but you know we couldn't do that; not now that we know…" She busied herself at the sink for a moment. "Well, you know."

"Yeah, I know," he told her and wished they'd change this subject, too.

Lisa straightened her shoulders and put on a bright smile. "Anyway, since Mom is gone, I feel it's my duty to hound you about your love life. You need to stop playing around and get serious with someone."

"And how do you know I wasn't serious before?"

She smiled at him as she placed some Cheerios on Lenny's tray. "Because I know you. You never go after them. It's like you don't want them to begin with. Each one walks out, and you go looking for another to replace her. You've been doing it your whole life. It's been this parade of life-sized Barbie dolls since high school. One of these days, you're going to have to settle down. And since I can't have a girl, I want a niece, and that leaves you to do your brotherly duty. If you have to, knock one of those girlfriends up. But *no more boys*."

Bryce could tell she was teasing him from the gleam in her brown eyes. She wouldn't seriously hope for him to get a woman pregnant just to get another girl in the family, would she?

He rolled his shoulders, shrugging off that thought. *Nah.* "Speaking of boys, where's Aaron?"

"Out with his father, fishing on the dock," she answered as she nodded out the kitchen window.

"How's he doing?"

Lisa sighed, looking worn out. She always looked worn out, but following her oldest son's diagnosis with Asperger's a few months ago, the life seemed to drain out of her quicker. "He's having a good week. He went to a birthday party last Friday. It took us the whole weekend to calm him down again."

He looked out the window at his six-year-old nephew sitting on the boat dock with his father, gripping a fishing pole as though his life depended on it. Bryce's heart squeezed with sorrow for his sister and her family. From the beginning, they all knew that Aaron was a strange child, even as a baby. They tried everything to get him to respond appropriately to the world around him, but they all feared the true reason for Aaron's odd behavior. Bryce thought the diagnosis was a few years too late.

Set against labeling her child, Lisa refused to have

Aaron tested when everyone else begged and pleaded with her. Bryce glanced over at his sister. She gazed lovingly at her oldest son and husband enjoying some precious one-on-one time. The last few years were hard on her, with the twins and now an eight-month-old baby, but she had eventually managed to regain some control over her life again. Not that she didn't constantly worry. One child with the disorder was enough to bear, but Bryce couldn't help noticing how her eyes strayed to her other three children as though waiting for a bomb to drop. Julian and Benji were not showing any signs – both very happy and well-adjusted children. That relieved Bryce. Still, he shared his sister's concerns...even if he didn't voice them.

What if his youngest nephew was diagnosed with Asperger's, or another kind of Autism? What if he himself had that gene and could give it to his own child?

"Sis, my offer still stands."

Lisa eyed him coolly. "Which offer is that again?"

He turned back to her. "Don't play coy with me. I can get you the best therapists in Dallas. A personal nanny who specializes in autism. Anything you need."

She smiled. "Thank you again, but no. This, we've decided to do on our own. Besides, you've already given me my dream home, and it's organized and labeled so that Aaron can function without much watching. I don't need anything else."

Bryce smiled as he studied the Cheerios on the floor under the baby and the chaotic spread of toys in the living room. "This is organized?"

Lisa laughed and swatted him with a dishtowel.

"You can leave anytime you want," she pointed out. "This is my house, if you haven't noticed."

That brought his mind back to the copyright problem. "Actually, there's something else I wanted to talk to you about. Remember that house in Grand Prairie you loved?"

"Yes," she said, mirroring his now stoic expression.

"Do you still have the paperwork on that?"

"What ever for? That architect guy was an A-S-S," she said, cupping her hands over Lenny's ears. "Surely you're not thinking of buying him out again?"

"No, it's just for a business issue that's come up. Do you still have it?"

She nodded, narrowing her eyes. "I think it's in the attic. We'll look for it after dinner. You are staying for dinner, right?"

He eyed the Cheerios again. "What are you making?"

She laughed. "I don't know yet. What do you want?"

He thought about that for a minute. His sister's cooking skills left a lot to be desired. He decided on something even she couldn't screw up. "Spaghetti."

"Homemade or canned?"

"Oh God, canned, please."

She laughed again and turned back to Lenny. Bryce left the kitchen and walked down to the dock, loosening his tie as he went. His brother-in-law, David, saw him coming and hopped up to greet him.

"Bryce. I didn't know you were coming out here today." He looked Bryce up and down, smirking at the tailored business suit. "You can't fish in that. Come on.

I've got some clothes in the boat house you can change into." David looked over Bryce's shoulder. "Is Kristen with you?" he whispered sourly.

Bryce sighed.

Two hours later, the men put away the fishing rods and studied their meager catch. "I hope Lisa wasn't expecting fish for dinner," David said quietly.

"No," Bryce replied. "I talked her into spaghetti."

David shot a look at him. "Homemade or canned?"

Bryce laughed out loud. Loud enough to scare Aaron, who had been reading the ingredients label on a can of bug spray, sounding out every syllable and mumbling about how the toothpaste in his bathroom had sodium fluoride in it, too. Bryce made a mental note to change toothpaste brands the next time he sent his housekeeper to the store.

~~~~~

"So what's this about house plans?" his brother-in-law asked, dropping his napkin on his empty dinner plate later that evening. David taught undergraduate level law at the University of Texas. He had a shrewd mind and waited until his wife had left the room to ask.

Bryce leaned his chair back to glance around the corner into the kitchen where his sister cleaned up her cooking mess. Lisa worried too much about him as it was. If she heard that he might be in some serious trouble...

"I bought a construction company out of Little Rock - Watson Construction. The houses that they build use designs similar to that one in Grand Prairie that Lisa liked so much."

"And?"

"And we have reason to believe that two different designers are claiming the same house plans."

"Fraud?"

Bryce shook his head. "I don't know yet. I'm just covering my bases. I don't want a legal case brought against us right now. I just need the sample plans from the architect in Grand Prairie for comparison. Henry Watson is a nice man, and his daughter claims the right to the plans I have in my possession. I don't want to upset anyone unnecessarily until I know if the plans match or not. It could be a mess, or it could be nothing."

David reclined, placing his hands behind his head. "With you, it's never just nothing."

"Seems that way, doesn't it? I'm flying to Little Rock tomorrow to talk to Lily Watson. Justin is handling the architect from Grand Prairie, if we can find him."

David scooted back his chair and rose. "Lisa said they were in the attic. Let's go look, shall we?"

Just after nine o'clock, Bryce stepped out of his sister's house, his suit covered in dust. But he had the paperwork he came for. "Do you have to go so soon? We never see you much anymore."

He kissed her cheek. "I've got an early flight in the morning. I'll drop by when I get back."

"Where are you going now? New York? Seattle? Ooh! Paris?"

"Little Rock," he answered with a grimace. The

heart of redneck country. He shrugged off that foul thought with a silent self-reprimand . Simple folk made up the glue of this country. He should know. He'd been simple once before. This must be the Barbie dolls talking.

Lisa gave him a sympathetic look, and then her eyes narrowed again. "Has this anything to do with that house?" She tapped the papers in his hand.

He hesitated. "Sis, do you still want that house?"

"I've always wanted it," she replied vaguely. "But this place is great, too. I've learned to settle with what I've got."

"I'll get you that house," he promised and left.

~~~~~

"I've got a new one," Bently said with a devious smile on Friday afternoon.

"Shoot," I said.

"What has no beginning, no end, and no middle?"

I frowned at him. "I still get a day, right?"

"Yup," he smiled around his barbeque sandwich. "One day, *no* help, or *you* host the next Movie Night."

"Alright," I huffed, glancing at my watch. "I'll call you by twelve-thirty tomorrow."

The shade of the puny oak tree, the only one left on the work site that was not situated by the lake, did not keep the burning sun from heating my skin as I ate my own lunch. "Tell me again why we had to cut down all the trees," I complained, staring up through the meager branches.

He grinned and bit into his sandwich. "Makes it easier to get the big trucks in. Surely you know that, boss lady."

"Stop calling me that," I growled, "and it should be a crime to remove every fully grown tree and then replace them later."

Bently kept his smile in place. "You could eat in the shack with your father. Nobody's making you sit out here with us mongrels."

I looked around at the mongrels. The Shepherd Brothers tussled on the ground nearby, and Delmar leaned against the tree trunk next to me with his eyes closed in a mid-day nap. The rest of the crew were camped out around a black pickup truck, listening to a replay of last night's Traveler's game.

"I don't want to be anywhere near that place. Daddy said Mr. King is coming in today."

"So you heard about that, huh?"

I sat up and glared at him. "What do you know?"

"Ah, come on, Lily. The place has been buzzing about it all morning. Everybody knows. Michael said something to Eddie, and there you go."

"Dang it, Michael. He's such an incurable gossip."

I grunted in exasperation, but I also smiled a little inside. These guys were all like brothers. It was kind of hard to stay mad at them for very long. Then melancholy swept over me as I foresaw the end of our little family. All thanks to Bryce King. Or Daddy…or whomever was responsible. I couldn't decide. I was mad at all of them.

A dark Mercedes rolled over the uneven dirt road

and stopped outside of the office building. All eyes turned that way. A rumbling cement truck or a flatbed tractor-trailer full of lumber, they'd never glance at, but this car screamed, "Rich, rich, and richer."

A few seconds later, a man dressed in an – *of course* – expensive, pinstriped suit stepped out. His reddish-brown hair glinted against the sunlight like little curls of aged copper. He had a classic, clean-shaven jaw with a small dimple, high cheekbones and a strong brow…and very sensual lips that smiled pleasantly, but his sunglasses hid his eyes. That was a shame.

Warmth spread through my limbs, and not from the sun. I pulled away from the feeling, wanting it to just go away, but it wouldn't, and I scowled at the newcomer who had caused it.

Bryce King. He looked younger than I imagined – not that I spent a whole lot of time thinking about what he'd look like.

Daddy bounded down the rickety stairs of the shack to meet our Mr. King. They shook hands and exchanged some words. Mr. King glanced around the work site quickly, pausing at my group under the tree. I felt his gaze pierce through me, and a jolt of that stupid warmth shot up my spine again.

"So that's Bryce King," Bently muttered with his easy-going smile. He turned to me. "He seems to like you, Lily."

"Nonsense," I said, shifting uneasily as Mr. King continued to stare at me. "Who wouldn't wonder at the only woman among all you mongrels?" I flashed him a smile and stood up, brushing the dirt from my jeans.

24

Something needed doing. Anything. I'd find something to do, even if I had to tear down a wall and build it up again. That man over there, now talking to Daddy again, made me nervous inside, and that irritated me further. So what if I was a dirty tomboy? I wasn't the first one to exist, and staring like that was just plain rude.

I set off away from the tree and Bently and Daddy's guest, and I did manage to find some work to do. I had to walk to the furthest site to find it, but it was there. Emilio and Andy were putting shovels to soaked ground, trying to dig out a muddy trench where a water pipe had leaked. I picked up a nearby shovel and joined in.

"Ah, Miss Lily," Emilio said in his broken English. "We not need help. You get dirty."

I planted my foot on the shovel and eyed him coolly. Andy kept his eyes on his work. Smart man. "Emilio, do I look like a woman who's afraid of a little dirt?"

He frowned at me curiously. "*¿No comprendo?*"

"Never mind," I waved at him with a grimy hand. "Let's get this done."

Half an hour later, with my anxiety and irritation finally sweated out of me and drenched to my knees in the brown blood of Mother Earth, Michael found me. "There you are. Why don't you have your radio?"

Because I didn't want to be found, I thought, but kept my mouth shut.

"Jesus, look at you," he said, and they all did. I gave him a look of pure steel. "You'd better get cleaned up. Mr. Watson wants to see you. You have to meet Mr. King."

I dropped my shovel and wiped the sweat off my brow. "I'm not going to get all dolled up for some fancy suit in a Mercedes. He can see me the way I am. I actually work for a living, and don't mind doing it." I strode off in the direction of the shack, feeling pretty good about my little speech. No man better mess with me now. Michael hurried to follow me as a worried frown hovered on his face.

Chapter Three

"That must be her now," Henry Watson said, rising to his feet as the outer door opened and slammed shut. A look of horror crossed the older man's face. "Christ, Lily! What have you been doing?" His daughter appeared in the small doorway, scowling as though she'd just finished chewing nails and spitting out barbed wire.

Lily Watson glanced at her father, ignoring Bryce. "Number eleven had a leak. I was helping Emilio dig out the pipe trench."

This is Lily Watson? Bryce stared at the woman. He remembered seeing her earlier when he arrived, but he would have never assumed the ragged, petite worker he saw outside was really a very talented – and possibly a very fraudulent – home designer. Mud covered her jeans and work boots, and she had a dark smudge on her forehead, where dirt and mud encrusted the wisps of hair that fell into her eyes. The rest of her dark brown mane hung down her back in a loose ponytail, and her eyes were so pale that the blue almost shone like crystals. Her tanned skin and muscular limbs did not seem to fit the china doll features of her face. Freckles were scattered across her nose, and a small scar stood out on her chin.

She was surreal.

Something unfamiliar and unwanted surged through his system. And he didn't like unfamiliar or unwanted. His gaze swept down her body, and Bryce forced his eyes away from the way her sweaty tank top clung to her breasts, a pair of perky, little things that begged for a man's attention...clothed or unclothed. When he looked up, he discovered her watching him. A small smile played in the corners of her lips. Full, pouty lips. He'd been caught, and she only smiled at him as though amused by the antics of a small child.

Bryce sat up straighter in his chair.

"You could have at least cleaned up a bit before coming in," Mr. Watson was saying. Lily turned her attention to her father and asked, "Why?"

"Why? Because we have a visitor."

"You've never cared before," she announced, dropping into one of the metal, folding chairs in front of the scarred, wood desk.

Mr. Watson sighed and said, "My apologies, Mr. King. Lily is a bit of a tomboy. She's been playing in the dirt since I could remember."

Lily tilted back in her chair and raised a dirty hand to him. "Nice to meechya, Mr. King."

He hesitated a moment before grasping her fingers, and she smirked at him. *Those lips.* "The pleasure is all mine," he managed to get out, quite proud of how cool his voice sounded.

She raised a shapely eyebrow. "He speaks."

"Lily," her father began. She directed that eyebrow at him, "Yes?"

Bryce realized that he still held her hand and he reluctantly let it go. Though her palms were rough and gritty, the skin on the outside of her hands felt as smooth as baby Lenny's cheeks. Bryce reclined in his own chair beside her, consciously aware of how she crossed her legs, lazily swinging a mud-encrusted boot.

Henry returned to his desk chair, glaring at his daughter.

"So Mr. King," she said to Bryce. "Why are you here?"

"I beg your pardon?"

Her father continued his heated glare, but allowed her to speak. Already, an interesting family dynamic took shape in Bryce's mind. The Watson's were close-knit and as plainspoken as they came.

"You already own the company. Why the visit? Guys like you don't usually take the time to visit every company you destroy, do you?"

Pouty lips or no, this woman had a bite, and it seemed her father gave her free reign over whom she chomped on. "A courtesy visit," Bryce replied smoothly.

"Courtesy, hmm. Do you use that word a lot, Mr. King? It sounds so callous when you say it."

"Lily, that's enough," her father finally commanded.

Bryce raised a hand. "No, Mr. Watson. Your daughter possesses a potent mind. She has the right to exploit it."

Henry Watson leaned back in his desk chair and gave him that "I warned you" look. Bryce ran a multi-million dollar business that employed thousands of people. Surely he could handle one little, mud-splattered girl. Even if her crystal gaze sent his pulse to pounding.

The girl rotated in her seat and bowed over the knees in a challenge. The neckline of her shirt dipped just enough to give him a peek of those tanned, little twin swells, but he was wise enough to appreciate them with only half an eye and kept the rest of his gaze on her face.

"What kind of *courtesy* visit?" she asked.

He smiled politely. "Occasionally, I like to check in on my investments. Get a feel for the environment."

"Investment?" she nearly roared with disbelief. "This is a family company, employing thirty-eight people on a regular work day. We're just chump change to a guy like you. So don't come at me with that suave corporate crap. Tell me why you are really here."

If she wasn't so damn magnetic to watch while she tore him up six ways to Sunday, he might be a little angry with her. But as it was, he was much too fascinated to feel anything else.

"No company is too insignificant. A chain is only as good as its weakest link." He folded his hands together in his lap and reclined casually into his chair's backrest, the epitome of complete ease. "I prefer to take personal interest in every part of my company."

Lily shook her head. "Only a man as rich as you can afford to say things like that."

Bryce curved his lips, hoping it looked like a smile. "Even the smallest ideas and principles have their worth, Ms. Watson. Take that house right there." He pointed to a drawing on the wall. "What would you say is the least important aspect of the design?"

Lily furrowed her brow as she studied the drawing. Bryce saw a spark of pride in her face, and he knew she drew it. "Nothing," she said, turning back to him. "Everything on the house is necessary. That's my parent's house, by the way, and I'm not sure if I like your insinuation."

"Insinuation?"

She closed her eyes with a tiny shake of her head. "Never mind. What's your point?"

"My point is that you can't tell me what's the least important factor," he replied calmly. "My company is the same. Even down to the lowest employee."

"And I suppose that would be everyone but you?" She grinned evilly at him. Her father groaned and stretched his fingers as if he wanted to wrap them around someone's throat.

Bryce kept his mind on the conversation, trying to find a way to avoid Mr. Watson's impending outburst at his daughter's behavior. "Do I hear a hint of malice, Ms. Watson?"

Okay, so he wasn't the best appeaser in the world.

"Yes!"

"Would you care to explain your malevolence toward me? I'm afraid I don't understand what I've done to upset you."

She crossed her arms in a huff, resembling a petulant teenager more than a full-grown woman. "Mr. King," she began in a hot voice, but her father cleared his throat and warned, "Lily…"

She clicked her teeth as she shut her mouth and looked away. Finally, she said, "I have no beef with you, Mr. King. Daddy says you're a fair man, and I have to trust that he's correct in his assumption."

Bryce didn't really care what Mr. Watson thought of him. He'd rather hear her piece of mind. "No, no," he said, "Please, tell me how you feel about me."

Her blue eyes met his for a loaded second, and

awareness bloomed in them under a tiny pleat in her mud-varnished forehead. Bryce reared back. Now, that was interesting.

However, she didn't voice her opinion, and her next words surprised him. "Mr. King, how much to do you make?"

"I beg your pardon?"

"Money," she explained, snapping her fingers at him, getting irritated again, and her father groaned again in disbelief. "What is your current worth?"

"Me? Or my company, Ms. Watson?"

"Just you, Mr. King. How much is in your personal bank accounts?"

Bryce drowned in the crystals of her eyes for a moment and saw that she was serious. Fascinated with her, mesmerized with the weird turn in conversation, he answered, "My quarterly statement put my personal accounts at around twelve point two million dollars."

She sucked in a quick breath, mouthed the figure he just threw at her, but kept the serious frown. "The last time I balanced my checkbook, I had eight hundred, fifty-six dollars, and I have yet to pay my mortgage—"

"Your mortgage?" he interrupted.

Lily smiled patiently. "Yes, Mr. King. My mortgage. It's that thing that us poor people pay to live in a house, in hopes that someday the bank will get its greedy little fingers off our wallets. I'm sure you haven't heard of it."

He returned the smile. "No, Ms. Watson. I meant, what is your mortgage?"

"Twelve hundred," she said, studying him for an underlying reason to his question. Her father pursed his lips together, and said, "I wish you would have told me, Lil Lil. I could have given you an advance."

Bryce glanced at Mr. Watson and made a mental note to have his accountant go over the company's books thoroughly. Employers shouldn't hand out advances for every sob story, even if that story was coming from his daughter. That was no way to run a business. He stifled his surprise as Lily said the exact same thing.

"Daddy, that's no way to run a business. You know that. I'll pay it on the next payday." Then she faced Bryce again, but he stopped her from her next snide remark, "A late mortgage is suicide for your credit score, Ms. Watson. I presumed you to be smarted than that."

"Unfortunately, I live in the real world, Mr. King. My credit score will just have to take a backseat to a roof over my head." She spoke calmly, but her muscles tensed. Her father closed his eyes, and the small room suddenly grew very warm with unspoken tension.

Am I missing something? Bryce wondered. "Again, I considered you to be smart enough to not buy a house you can't afford."

For just a second, her clear eyes flashed blue fire, and Henry dropped his head into his hands with another groan. Bryce thought that if he had a daughter like Lily Watson, he'd be groaning a lot, too.

"When I built the house, Mr. King, I could afford it. I had some help," she said, too calmly. Much too calmly.

"Had?"

"Yes. Had." The tone of her voice and the sickly pallor of Mr. Watson warned Bryce to drop the subject. But what the hell? He like the way her crystal eyes glinted when she was angry. It was enchanting. *She* was enchanting.

"And what happened to your help?"

She delivered one very long, even look and stood up. "I don't believe that my personal life is any of your business, Mr. King. Now if you will excuse me, I have a job to do."

Lily Watson stormed out of the little office building, and Henry winced as the door slammed behind her.

"Charming girl you have," Bryce muttered.

"You have no idea."

Bryce turned toward the older man, who studied him with curiosity. "Mr. King," Henry began, "Lily did have a point, well, before she got off-subject. Why are you here, exactly? Was there something wrong with the contract?"

Bryce decided to stick to the truth, or at least, part of it. "My associate, Justin Barker, reviewed your company's files. Justin has a nose for valuable assets. And as you are aware, my initial interest in Watson Construction was based on a favor for our mutual friend, Vivian. You wanted to sell, and she owned stock in a corporation that I wanted. Vivian would sell her shares, if I agreed to acquire your company."

Henry nodded his head, "Yes, I know all that. But why the personal visit?"

"Going back to my associate, Justin. He is the one who piqued my interest. Justin discovered a sort of treasure in your company. The house plans used for this particular development." Bryce watched for any anomaly in Henry's expression. There was nothing more than an unusual brightening of pride.

"Of course," the older man said. "I knew Lily's plans would finally catch someone's attention. She's very talented."

And intriguing. But Bryce kept that thought locked away.

"So these are Lily's houses that you are building?"

"Oh yes," Henry nodded eagerly. "She designed the software that develops the plans some years ago. It took us a long time to get an investor—"

"Vivian," Bryce inserted.

"Right. Vivian saw the potential from the start. Come," he said, standing, "I'll show you the model home and then you can see for yourself."

Bryce was much more interested in seeing this software, but Henry ushered him out into the summer sun and around the back of the portable building to where a battered Gator sat parked. They drove out to the gated entrance. A large, two-story Cape Cod style home with a perfectly manicured lawn stood gleaming in the sunshine. Bryce noticed it on his way into the work site, but didn't pay much attention to it. It was a normal rectangular home with symmetrical windows and brown brick. Nothing special, really.

Henry led him into the front room, and immediately Bryce sensed a difference. He looked around the furnished, unused rooms, trying to find the source of the discrepancy. Henry grinned.

"You understand, don't you? I can see it on your face. Just a normal house, right? But you feel something's different, don't you? That's called 'potential.'"

Bryce walked into the living area. An open kitchen filled the back half of the giant room, and finally, he did understand. The house had potential -potential to be anything he wanted. Ideas stormed through his head. The kitchen could be a little bigger, and the stairs should curve the other way...a bathroom here...an arched opening...patio doors there...

And every alteration seemed so easy to accomplish, as if the house itself created a new design inside his head.

"Come," Henry was saying, "I'll show you part of the real genius." He waved Bryce to another room that could be used as an office or a guest room. Along one wall, a few tables held a display of home plans and a few miniature models.

Bryce went immediately to the models, studying each one. Besides the Cape Cod model, a Colonial, a Craftsman and a Tudor graced the long table. Four completely different style homes, and yet they all looked as if they belonged together. Colors, brick patterns, slight variations of angles and roof pitches...

"Look here," Henry directed him, excitement dripping from his voice. Bryce turned to another table. One of the house plans had been cut up into the various rooms, and a box of more room cutouts sat nearby.

Henry scooted pieces around, creating a totally different home, moving the living areas, bathrooms, and bedrooms into new formations. Bryce watched with fascination. A vision of a house came to him as he observed the new plan. He flipped through the other rooms, choosing a few that stood out to him. He shuffled the rooms around, placing them just how he pictured his house. Then he stood back, quietly contemplating the situation.

Potential.

That one word pinpointed the allure of these homes. With these cutouts, a person could design his own dream home. Almost anything you wanted with one set of plans.

"It's the computer program, really," his companion explained. "The genius of Lily's idea is the program. She designed it so that the buyer plays around with designs, and then the program puts all the pieces together to form a working blueprint. A lot of architectural firms use similar software, but Lily's is easy enough for the average Joe to figure out. Every home in this development was designed by the new homeowners, right down to the type of brick on the walkways. In a couple of hours, a person can own the blueprint to their very own dream home. The success of this development will launch Lily's software into the open market. A person can make a fortune off it."

So far, Bryce had not uttered a word since entering the model home. How could he? The dollar signs in his eyes muddled anything he could possibly say. Bryce shook his head clear. One promise he had made to himself and to his sister was that he would not become blinded by money. He would remember who he was, and where he came from. People came first in his companies.

Oh, but the *potential!*

He focused on the older man. "Who owns the rights to the software?"

Henry's reply was slow to come. "The company does."

"Not Lily?"

"No, she signed over rights to the company to secure the development contract."

"So, now I own it?"

Henry sighed, "Yes. I'm afraid Lily hasn't come to that conclusion yet. She'll be furious, of course."

"And no one else has the right to it?"

"No." Henry answered slowly again.

"What if the software spits out a design similar to another architect?"

"There's no legal repercussion, if that's what you're thinking. The software uses a legal waver. The homeowners must sign off on it before they can use it. It's all in the paperwork I sent you last month."

Bryce thought about Nicholas Garcia, and wondered if he once had access to Lily's software and was now passing off designs from it as his own. Was that legal?

Mr. Watson studied Bryce. He said, "No one else owns a copy of the software or the original plans. Lily received everything in the divorce."

Bryce's eyes narrowed considerably. "Divorce?"

The older man let out a long breath. "Yeah, she'll kill me for telling you this, but Lily was married for nine months. The guy was scum. He cheated on her, stole from me, got involved in some shady investments. Anyway, she divorced him and instead of pressing charges against him, he signed over any right to their assets." He glanced at Bryce with a half smile. "Don't let on that you know anything. I do have to see her from time to time."

Bryce nodded. "I will have to investigate the matter further. I want to make sure that there are no other claims to my property."

"I understand. I just ask that you keep it quiet."

"I'm sure I can handle that. What is the name of Lily's ex-husband?"

"Nicolas Garcia."

Chapter Four

My hiding places were getting harder to find. After leaving Daddy's office, I scurried toward the model home, needing to get away from curious eyes and Bryce King's handsome face. Once inside the house, a glance in the hall mirror displayed why he'd looked at me with such amused eyes.

A flaking smear of dried mud covered my forehead and part of my hairline, chipping off in little patches. Another splatter sat upon my chin, and a thick layer of dust finished the picture. I groaned, sounding more like Daddy than I desired, and wished I had taken Michael's advice to clean up first. I would never be an eye-catching beauty, but at least I would have looked female.

Quickly washing my face in the kitchen sink, I thought over the meeting with Bryce King and wondered why I hadn't kept my mouth shut during most of it. But there was just something about that man that bothered me. Maybe it was his height. Even though he never stood up, I could gauge it for myself. I was consciously aware of the fact that the top of my head probably only came to his jaw, making me look like a child.

Growing up, I acquired the nickname, Lil Lil, short for Little Lily, after one especially torturous and teasing Thanksgiving when I was six. My sister, Marissa, stood tall and willowy, like a supermodel. But I didn't get that gene. On a good day, I could claim five feet, two inches, and I would never be called willowy. Slender, but solid, that's me.

Luckily, I managed to keep a layer of baby fat that rounded out the muscular angles of my body and gave me something akin to breasts. Otherwise, I may as well tattoo *I really was born a girl* on my forehead.

The rumble of the Gator broke my thoughts. I glanced out a window and saw Daddy and Mr. King coming this way. I muttered a curse and darted out the backdoor a step before they entered the house.

Damn, he's gorgeous, I thought, and hurried to find another spot away from the questions I knew were brewing in everybody's mind. Eddie and Bently spotted me and started in my direction with mouths open, ready to interrogate me about Mr. King. I quickly turned away and ran across the barren yards of neighboring house structures.

Bryce King. Not the type of man I usually felt attracted to. I liked them blonde, athletic, and dumb. Men were easier to manage that way; cute, good in bed, and not smart enough to use it against you.

But Mr. King was anything but those three things. Reddish hair, tall and lean, but not with that athlete build, and definitely not dumb. He had those classic, good-old boy features mixed with savvy shrewdness as though he heard and saw every word and movement around him, dissecting it, memorizing it, and filing it away for future study. Bryce King was not the easily managed kind of man and a nightmare for girls like me.

Girls like me weren't cut out to cope with sexy, rich men. Girls like me, born with the grit of the earth in our veins and the tangy aroma of pine trees in our lungs, didn't have the stamina to endure relationships with men like Bryce King. He had sophistication written all over that fancy suit – no matter what Daddy said about his "humble" beginnings. Mr. King and men like him weren't dreams come true…they were nightmares, plain and simple. Nightmares that would break a country girl's heart if she wasn't careful.

And I'm very careful.

~~~~~

All I could think about as I darted from site to site, looking for one that was empty of workers, was hiding. But every time I darted into a house, the Gator followed right after me. Once I thought I saw Mr. King glance in my direction as I rounded a corner of the next house, but I could just be imagining things.

Site ten, the last house on this side of the street, was deserted, waiting on the stonemason scheduled to arrive on Monday. I slithered into the backdoor and up the stairs, hoping nobody saw me. In the master bedroom, which had recently gotten a coat of plaster on the walls, the balcony doors opened to let in fresh air and a stunning view of the little lake. The afternoon August sun glinted off the water, winking up at me as tiny ripples marred the otherwise glassy surface. The house, though unfinished, already had a dock, and I mulled over going down there to dip my feet in the water. I had dived off that dock a few times already, into the lake to cool off after a long, torturous day of hauling around building equipment.

My skin began to itch as the sweat dried and the

dust and mud flaked off. I checked my watch and sighed. There was still four hours left in the workday. I couldn't very well strip down to my underwear while male eyes surrounded me.

The unmistakable sound of Daddy's Gator jerked me upright. Did I have a tracking device on me somewhere? *Shoot!*

I scurried down the balcony stairs and galloped across the sloped lawn towards the lake. Peeking around the tiny storage shed on the end of the dock, I saw Mr. King and Daddy emerge onto the balcony, Daddy gesturing animatedly about the lake. Even from afar, Bryce King looked too handsome for my own good.

They couldn't see me, so I took off my work boots, rolled up the cuffs of my jeans and lowered my body down to sit on the edge of the dock. I sighed as the cool water covered my sore feet. A girl could get used to this kind of break in her schedule. I should have been over on site six, slapping mud on the new wallboards, but the guys could handle it for a while longer. As the site manager, I could slack off for a few minutes if I wanted to and let a guilty conscience steal over me, the heat of my shameful rest competing with the coolness of the water.

Time slowed down. I closed my eyes and lifted my face to the summer sun. So immersed in the serenity of the moment, I didn't hear the tread of patent leather shoes behind me.

"May I join you?"

His smooth voice broke through my tranquility, and, as I twisted around to face Bryce King, my bottom lost its perch on the dock, and I fell sideways into the lake. Water filled my mouth and nose as I screeched. The lake was only a little more than five feet deep here, but I had to kick to the surface, sputtering to clear my throat and nasal passages. A hand reached down and grabbed a hold of my arm; hauling me out of the water with no more effort than if I had been a rag doll.

"Are you okay?"

I pushed my wet hair out of my face . *Well, at least I'm not muddy anymore.* I glared at the intruder. "I'm just *peachy*," I said vehemently.

"And wet," Mr. King added with a grin. *Lord, don't grin like that.*

"And it's entirely your fault."

"I didn't drag you down here and toss you into the lake, Ms. Watson. You fell in. I am free of all blame on this one."

I jerked out of his grasp. "Do you normally carry around a guilty conscience?"

He shrugged. "Not usually. It is comparatively clean."

"Is there a reason you are here, Mr. King?" I dropped to the dock to pull on my work boots. Hell...what was the point? I couldn't go back to work like this anyhow. I stood and picked up the boots by the laces.

He sighed and smiled politely. "Please, Ms. Watson, call me Bryce."

I glared at him again. "I would never call my boss by his first name."

"Only my secretary calls me Mr. King, and I've been

trying to get her to stop for years." I crossed my arms, the boots swinging wide and hitting him in the arm. He didn't seem to notice and I didn't apologize.

"Okay, Bryce," I agreed.

"May I call you Lily? Or is that too forward?"

"Too forward for what?"

His mouth tipped up secretly. "If you need to ask, I'll assume that it's not important."

My head cocked to the side as I asked, "Do you always talk in riddles?"

Bryce shook his head. "I repeat my question. May I call you Lily?"

"Lily is fine." I edged around him. The heat of the day amplified the scent of his cologne as it wafted toward me. He smelled...spicy. Male. And I forced myself to stop breathing before I stuck my nose to his neck and inhaled the life out of him.

"Are you leaving me here all alone, Lily?"

"I have work to do," I said, hoping he wouldn't point out my drenched state.

"Then I'll see you tonight."

I came to a standstill halfway up the long dock. "Tonight?"

"Yes," he said a step behind me. "Your father invited me over for dinner tonight. He said you would be there as well."

"Did he now?"

His grin showed even, white teeth...the kind that could sink into an earlobe and fire untold pleasures down a woman's spine. "Yes, he most certainly did. Am I to guess that you had other plans?"

"Um…"

"Because I hoped we might have a moment to talk." He casually stuffed his hands into his pants pockets and tilted his head, causing those burnished curls on his head to fall over his brow.

"Talk?" I squeaked. Gracious, I needed to get away from him. I looked like a drowned rat. He was a lot taller than I imagined, and I didn't particularly like squinting up at him, looking into those dark eyes that now appeared to have a good bit of hunter green in them. I just wanted to be away from him and his expensive clothes.

"Yes, we need to talk."

"About what?"

He blinked down at me for a moment. Then I heard a loud boom coming from one of the sites, accompanied by a symphony of shouts and curses. I pivoted on my socked feet and ran toward the newest catastrophe, silently thanking whoever was responsible for giving me a reason to leave Bryce on the dock.

"It was a pleasure to meet you, Lily," he called after me. "I'll see you later." My pace picked up and I hit the grass at full speed. Bryce's voice held a ton of promise in that last sentence. What in the world did he want to talk about? And why on earth did my father invite that man to dinner? Wasn't this one afternoon enough visiting for one day?

Daddy, you've finally lost your marbles!

~~~~~

"Justin, tell me you have some good news," Bryce said into his cell phone.

"Sorry, Bryce. Nicolas Garcia has disappeared. No one has seen him since last week sometime."

"Is there a missing person's report out on him?"

"Only the one I filed this morning. Apparently, what little family Mr. Garcia has is not aware of his disappearance."

"Just peachy," Bryce murmured, throwing his body backward on the king-sized bed.

"What?" Justin asked. "Did you just say 'peachy'?"

Bryce laughed into the phone. "Yeah, I did."

"Where did you hear *that* word?"

"I learned it from Lily Watson today." He smiled up at the ceiling, remembering the way her lake-soaked t-shirt clung to her body. Once the mud and dirt washed away, the glow of her tanned skin made the pale clarity of her blue eyes even more apparent. He got a little hot again just thinking about her.

"Speaking of which," Justin continued. "I learned something interesting about Lily Watson."

"She was married to Nicolas Garcia," Bryce filled in for him.

"Damn," his friend muttered, "How do you do that so fast? I just found out not ten minutes ago."

"What else did you learn?"

"Nothing. Besides the fact that Garcia walked away from that marriage with nothing but the clothes on his back, and damn lucky to have those. From the divorce documents I'm reading now, this Ms. Watson is a cougar. She took everything."

"Does it mention anything about the house plans or a software program?" Bryce rolled over to adjust some pillows behind his head. The pillows were soft and smelled vaguely feminine, like Lily might fresh out of a shower.

He erased that image from his mind. He'd never get to see Lily emerging from a steamy shower. No sense in dwelling on the possibilities.

"Not a word. All it says is that he declined his right to any asset acquired during the time of marriage." Justin grunted and the sound of shuffling papers came through the phone. A baby's shriek followed. Bryce smiled. Justin worked from his home office more than from the downtown office due to his and his wife's new arrival. A hazy ache settled in Bryce's chest.

"It's this design software we need to concentrate on," Bryce said. "Go back through the documents on the construction company and look over the legalities of that computer program. We need to know if Garcia used plans developed through that program and passed them off as his own creations. I want to know if he used any plans during, before or after the marriage."

"You still want me to look for Garcia?" Justin asked.

"Yeah. I didn't like the guy when I met him the first time. Mr. Watson told me some interesting things about him, and I want him questioned."

"Will do," Justin said, his voice slightly muffled by the cooing of his daughter.

Bryce rolled his head on the pillow and looked at the bedside clock. He had about two hours until his dinner at the Watson's house. The directions were in his pocket, but they lived in a little community across the river called Maumelle. Henry said that traffic could be bad this time of day. He'd have to add some travel time if he didn't want to be late.

"You still there, man?"

"What?" he answered with a start. "Oh, yeah, I'm here. I've got to go. I'm having dinner at the Watson's tonight."

"Lily going to be there?"

"Why?" The short question came out too sharply, and his friend noticed.

Justin chuckled, "Hey, I'm just asking. I'm looking at a wedding photo. She's a looker, that's for sure." Justin hummed for a moment, and Bryce assumed that he was calming his baby, but then he said, "She's kind of short, though."

"You have no idea," Bryce said.

"The short part, or the looker part?"

"Never mind," he said, sitting up. "You got anything else for me?"

"Nope. I'll call you when I do. When are you flying back?"

"I don't know yet. This weekend at the latest."

"Alright then. You want me to schedule a tetanus shot for Monday? You never know what you might bring back from the land of *Deliverance*." Justin snickered at his own joke.

"Funny, Justin. I'll call you tomorrow." Bryce ended his call and hopped in the shower.

~~~~~

Just before six o'clock, he parked his rented Mercedes outside the Watson's house. It was just like the drawing in Henry's cramped office at the work site, a Colonial reproduction overlooking the third green of a nine-hole golf course neighborhood. His stomach clenched. How long had it been since he swung his Callaway driver? Three days? Four? He never seemed to find enough time to indulge any more.

"You must be Mr. King," a silky voice said from behind him. He hadn't realized that his feet had ferried him into the backyard of the Watson's home, the sloping lawn fading into rough and then to fairway.

A taller, more graceful version of Lily rocked in a nearby patio swing, hidden from the house's view by a barrier of rose bushes. He turned and smiled broadly – *Hello, Beautiful* – until his eye caught the glint of a wedding ring. Now, that was just a crime; to take this lovely creature out of the dating pool.

A screen door slammed. "Marissa? You out here?"

Lily rounded the bushes, still dressed in jeans, but clean ones, and a black, knit top that was held up with nothing more than two straps tied behind her neck. And she wasn't wearing a bra. He could tell that much from where he stood.

Lily stopped when she spotted him. "Oh, Mister-" she hesitated as if remembering, "uh, I mean, Bryce. You're here."

"I am here," he confirmed with an amused smile.

Her annoyed mask slid into place as she fiddled with the neckline of her shirt. The soft material slid over her

50

breasts, making the nipples stand erect and point straight at him. "Then meet my sister," Lily said. "Marissa, this is Bryce King."

Marissa raised her hand and arched an eyebrow at the flush in his cheeks. A tiny, laughing glimmer entered her eyes. "Pleasure to meet you, Mr. King."

He grasped her hand, averting his gaze from Lily's points of interest and her sister's knowing glint. "It's Bryce."

"Bryce," the sister mused, lazily kicking the swing into motion with her foot. Lily cleared her throat, and Bryce noticed that he still held Marissa's hand.

"BoBo called," Lily informed her sister in an oddly tight voice. "He wants to know when you're coming home." Marissa pulled her hand away from him and stood.

"Is Bri ready?" Marissa asked.

"Almost," Lily answered , and then backed up onto the brick patio, gaining her another three inches of height. Bryce considered that. Now he realized that he could normally see the top of her head without straining. Lily really was short. *Hmm*...unless he thought about it, he just didn't notice. Her presence was so forward and looming.

"Well, Bryce, you may as well come in," Lily was telling him. He gave the fairway one last, longing look and followed Lily and Marissa through the back door.

"Isn't your sister staying for dinner?" he asked Lily when they stopped in a large kitchen. Marissa disappeared into another part of the house.

"No," Lily spit out. "She has to go home to her

husband."

"Who's Bri?" he asked, confused at her sudden animosity. What'd he do now?

She rounded on him, lifting her chin as she glared up at him. "Are you always this nosy?"

He considered her question. "Yes."

"Marissa's step-daughter," she answered, now amused at the thought of something that had nothing to do with him. With him, she was always annoyed for some reason. Muffled shouts filtered through the house. Lily took a step toward the sound, but stopped, shaking her head and muttering, "Stay out of it, Lily."

"Stay out of what?" he asked, just to see that flare of irritation again. It made her blue eyes shine so wonderfully.

"What?"

He stuck his hands into the front pockets of his khaki pants and grinned. "Normally, I prefer to stay out of others' domestic problems, but I'm fascinated. What's going on in there?"

Lily blinked hotly at him.

A few seconds later, the shouting grew louder, the front door slammed with a window-rattling force, and Marissa rushed into the kitchen, looking pale and angry. "Sorry, Lil Lil, she's in a mood today. I'll call you later." She gave her shorter sister a quick hug and turned to Bryce, "So nice to meet you, Bryce. I apologize for the racket." Then she was gone.

Lily stilled her face with difficulty and said, "Bri has recently been un-grounded, and she's testing her boundaries again. I guess it's safe to enter the rest of the house."

"You don't approve of your niece's behavior," he said, and not as a question.

"I don't approve of how *a lot* of people behave, Mr. King, but I try not to stick my nose into it either."

He couldn't help wondering if that comment was a jab at him or not. She took his arm, guiding him through the kitchen, a small skip in her step. From annoyed to amused in ten seconds flat. This woman was something else.

Somehow, he got the feeling this would be an unusual night.

Chapter Five

I *really should learn to listen to my intuitions more,* he thought after dinner was over and he withdrew to the edge of the fairway in the Watson's backyard. He'd earned a strong business sense the hard way and was quite proud of his ability to sniff out good deals and even better prospects. But when it came to his social sense around this quirky family, he knew he was lacking.

The actual meal was great. Nomi Watson cooked like a goddess, sending him back to his childhood summers when he visited his grandparents' ranch outside of San Antonio. He hadn't eaten this good of a home-cooked meal since he'd been a teenager. Nomi, the beautiful, down-to-earth matriarch, kept the conversation alive during dinner, but, at times, Bryce wondered if he'd somehow stumbled into a tennis match. His neck ached from the back and forth motion of Henry and Lily's recurrent bickering.

In fact, sitting next to Lily and across from Nomi could have been a wet dream come true. Lily's thigh brushed his shoulder once when she left her seat for a second bottle of wine, and he'd almost sighed at the warmth of that succulent, muscular limb rubbing against him. And the view in front of him was pretty damn good, too. Lily got her eyes from her mother, and those same china doll features on a mature woman made him jealous of Henry Watson. But there was just something about Lily that drew his eye to her whenever she spoke. The animation in her face intrigued him to the point of an addiction. He could watch her talk all night long.

Other than that, the night started out fairly normal,

until Lily slapped the table, making the silverware jump, and shrieked, "Oh my God! A doughnut!"

All eyes turned to her, and she burst out laughing so hard and loud that she fell back against her chair, causing it to scoot across the hardwood floor. She ended up on her butt under the table, where she hit her head on a chair rung. Bryce looked at Henry for an explanation, but the older man put his head in his hands and just groaned. Nomi bent her head under the table, lifting the tablecloth, and calmly asked, "Lil Lil, are you alright, dear?"

Lily crawled into her chair, a huge, captivating grin on her petite face. "I'm fine."

"No more wine for you," her mother said, moving the wine bottle out of her daughter's reach. Lily propped up in her seat, placing her napkin in her lap and sipped her wine glass with a tolerant expression, as though nothing happened.

Bryce stared at her. Yes, there was something about this woman that got to him.

Almost an hour after Lily's outburst, he stood squinting against the setting sun in the Watson's backyard. Nomi shooed him out the door when he offered to clean up the dinner mess. Which was fine with him. He'd rather curl up on that Bermuda grass out there on the fairway and watch the sun go down on this day. Lily came up behind him with a two tall tumblers of iced-tea, handing one it to him.

"Thank you," he said.

"You're welcome," she replied, waving her glass at the golf course. "Do you play?"

"Golf, or just play in general?"

She ignored his teasing and asked, "What's your handicap?"

"Eleven. Yours?"

She arched an eyebrow at him. "You assume I play?"

He glanced at her muscular limbs and the sure way she stood next to him on the edge of the fairway lawn, and he knew she did. "Yes. I assume. What is your handicap?"

"Ten and a half," she answered with a smile.

"That sounds like a challenge."

She took a swallow of tea, and he liked the way her throat undulated under her chin. "I like a good challenge," she said, licking the drink off her bottom lip. Bryce's eyes zeroed in on the pink tip of her tongue. "Daddy has a tee-time at seven-thirty, tomorrow morning. You can join us, if you're still here." She cringed delicately, like she regretted offering.

"I'm afraid I didn't bring my bag with me this trip."

"That's okay," she said. "Daddy keeps a spare set for visitors. They're not PGA worthy, but they'll get you to the green."

"What do you use?"

"No," she shook her head. "I'm not going to answer that."

"Why not?"

"Because you probably spent more money on your driver, than I did on my entire set. If you play badly tomorrow, I'll attribute it to you using Daddy's mediocre clubs, and I won't respect you because you have to hide behind your equipment to get results - and that's just wrong. Golf is like great sex. If you need expensive toys to total up a winning scorecard, you're not doing it right." She drank from her glass again, viewing his reaction over the rim.

A flash of Lily in the midst of sex seized his brain, but he ignored it – and the tightening of his pants – and smiled politely at her. "It never hurts to know your shaft won't bend and throw off your swing."

Her eyes widened briefly, more of that awareness flaring in those blue depths, and then she returned the smile. "And I suppose your technique is to 'grip it and rip it'?"

"Actually," he said, stepping closer to her. "I'm a student of simplicity. I like a balanced stance and an interlocking grip." He inched closer; his voice lowered. "I prefer to take my time and concentrate on finding just the right spot on the fairway, rather than pounding out a drive that goes long and wrong."

His next step brought him close enough to feel the warmth of her body, radiating off in waves, and to see the reflection of the sunset in her clear eyes. Her lips parted as he resumed, "And I have discovered that if I relax and enjoy myself, I finish every round with my balls accounted for and a scorecard I'm proud of."

She blinked at him, her lashes fanning the glow of her stunned expression. And for a second, he considered kissing her. Her pouty lips would be sweet as honey, her body welcoming in his embrace. But she stumbled back a step, putting space between them.

"And to think, I was just beginning to wonder if we

had anything in common at all," she said.

"Why shouldn't we?" he asked, gaining control of his urges. "We're both human beings, incorporated into this world together."

She sighed and shook her head. "And then you go and say words like 'incorporated.'"

"What is wrong with 'incorporated'?"

"Just that normal people don't talk like that. At least not around here. We're simple folk, using simple words. We don't need fancy vocabulary to make our point." She swallowed the rest of her tea and meandered back toward the yard. He followed her like a lost puppy, and he was disgusted with himself because of it, and intrigued by her for making him feel this way. She sat on the swing by the rose bushes, her feet barely brushing the ground under her.

His feet stopped in front of the swing. "Then, tell me, Ms. Watson. How would you describe our relationship? In your simple words?"

She glanced up at him, sighed again, and patted the seat next to her. "Sit, Bryce. You're giving me a crick in my neck."

He eyed the spot beside her body. The swing was barely big enough for two people, and sitting so close to her would remind him of how he almost considered kissing her. Not that he needed much reminding. But hell, he was a man who took risks, and enjoyed it. He lowered himself onto the swing, kicking it into motion.

"First of all, *we* don't have a relationship," she began, waving a finger back and forth, nearly poking him in the nose. "And second, people are like dots, scattered all over a sheet of paper. By themselves, they are just dots. But if you draw a line between each and every dot, you get a web – a tangled mess." Her finger traced imaginary shapes in the air. "To some people, that mess could be a magnificent work of art. A masterpiece of human interactions. To others, it's just a mess. Complete chaos. And it's up to each person to describe their web one way or the other."

Bryce blinked at her. *Say what?*

He cleared his throat. "So, which are you, Lily? An art critic or a mess maker?"

"Me?" she inquired, her face grinning and shining and so tempting that he thought about kissing her again. "I'd like to be the critic, but I know I'm probably just part of the mess."

He knew he was in a mess. "And me?"

Her grin split her face. "You, Bryce King, are a dot, plain and simple."

"A dot?" He smiled back at her. "So, I'm not part of the world?"

"You like to think you are, but rich people don't tangle with rubbish."

He knew he should have felt annoyed about that, but her eyes were shining with such humor that he couldn't muster the irritation. "I wasn't always just a dot. I've been twisted and tangled before."

Her gaze swept over him. "Yes, I can imagine you were, but it doesn't matter what you were. It's what you are that counts. And you are a dot."

Arguing with her was a luxury he decided to forgo for the moment. He'd like to end the night on a positive note. "A dot," he agreed.

~~~~~

If I keep holding my breath around him, I'm going to pass out and then he'd have to give me mouth to mouth...

God! Don't think about that!

He smelled so good, and looked so good, and would probably taste so good. My eyes flicked to his mouth. Sweet Lord, this wasn't right. This man was way out of my league. He watched my face, and as the silent seconds ticked by, his got a little bit closer.

"Momma baked an apple pie for desert," I offered, jumping to my feet and away from him. What was I thinking when I told him to sit next to me? The man's cologne emitted something delicious, decadent, and expensive – much too rich for me.

Bryce King better not be a dunce on the fairway tomorrow, or my Me-Time fantasies for the next decade would be ruined. And I'd got some dizzies already stored up for later tonight, involving scorecards and carving out a few extra divots. It bothered me that those fantasies came so quickly with Bryce. Until now, my favorite had been a blonde version of a sweaty gladiator, all decked out in his leather warrior gear.

Oh, Lordy! I fanned myself with my fingers. All that bronzed, muscular flesh, flaunted in the bright sunlight. A sword flashing, sweat dripping down his chest, dark green eyes glinting with hot, savage lust...

I glanced back at Bryce, pictured him in a leather

skirt and shin guards, and immediately turned back around. He followed me into the house, not noticing the flush of my cheeks, but his eyes widened at the sight of Momma and Daddy sitting on the little sofa by the breakfast nook – or rather, Momma sat, hiked up on Daddy's lap. Her muffled giggles could be heard from the neighbor's house. Momma's skirt rode high due to Daddy's wandering hands, and I was pretty sure Bryce caught a glimpse of where I once resided.

Jeez! Not again.

My parents' unabashed, intimate relationship caused a lot of awkward moments in my lifetime. This episode paled in comparison to the night when Mickey O'Doole picked me up for our senior prom, so, nowadays, I was pretty much immune to it all. But Bryce was not. He whipped around quickly, took my elbow, and *dragged* me into the dining room around the corner. "Hey," I protested, snatching my arm back. Okay, not more gladiator fantasies. Way too rough.

"Sorry," he whispered, "I didn't want to embarrass them, walking in like that."

"Embarrass who?" I asked, rubbing my elbow.

He gazed down at me, a small frown forming on his lips. "Mr. and Mrs. Watson were-"

"Were what?"

His frown vanished, replaced by a curious smile. "Well, they were…" He shrugged, unable to find the words, and then *he* looked embarrassed, yet faintly amused by something.

"Oh, for crying out loud," I said and walked back to the kitchen. "Momma, Daddy, cut it out." Daddy looked up from tackling the buttons on Momma's blouse. "Bryce is uncomfortable," I informed them and took the pie out of the oven.

Momma rose to her feet, completely unashamed as she smoothed down her skirt. "Oh, dear. I am sorry, Mr. King. That was rude of us." She fixed her shirt and helped gather plates from the cabinet.

"You missed a button," I told her, grinning as Bryce slowly emerged from the dining room.

"It is I who should apologize," he said. "I did not intend to interrupt your, um, conversation." He sat at the breakfast table, clearly out of his element here, and a mischievous urge shot through me.

"Bryce," I said sweetly, and my tone caught his attention. His eyes narrowed a fraction. "My parents are pretty open about their physical relationship." He winced delicately; I set a pie slice in front of him and leaned over on my elbows, getting right in his face. "And if you are uncomfortable about that…"

"I am not uncomfortable," he said warily.

"Oh, good," I said, "then you won't mind eating at this particular table."

"I beg your pardon?"

I grabbed the edge and shook it. The table rocked noticeably on loosened leg joints. "Let's just say, it didn't used to wobble."

He scooted back, staring, appalled at me and the table. Momma slapped me on the back of my head, "Stop being rude, Lil Lil. Let the man eat."

"Jesus, Lily," Daddy snorted. "The man is your boss. Show some decency."

"You two are the ones necking in the corner with a guest in the house. And besides, he is not my boss," I told him. "You said so yourself."

Bryce held up a finger, "On the contrary. Since you have not been dismissed, and have not filed a resignation, I am indeed your boss."

I crossed my arms under my breasts. "Fine. Fire me."

"I can't," Bryce said, digging into his slice of pie. "You are under contract. I do not fire indiscriminately, and since you are not presently working, what you do or say during your free time is your business."

"Even if I say it to your face?"

"Lily," my father warned, and Momma slapped me again.

"Stop doing that!"

Bryce looked at the three of us, shook his head, and ate his pie.

"What now?" I asked him.

"Nothing, Lily," he said. "I shall keep my opinions to myself."

"Very wise of you," Momma told him.

"How is that wise?" I rounded on her. "How can people improve if no one shares their opinions with each other?"

"That's not what I meant, dear. I only meant to say that it was wise of him to not share his opinions with you."

Bryce grinned around his fork, and I opened my mouth to retort, but my cell phone jingled the tune "Little Girls" from my back pocket. I sneered at all of them as I answered the call.

"*Hello,*" I growled.

"So is it true?" my best friend, Ann, said through the phone. I backed around the kitchen island and turned away from inquiring eyes. Momma and Daddy exchanged a look and announced, "Ann."

"Who?" Bryce wondered. I didn't hear my parent's explanation because Ann was still talking.

"Bently told me that your dad sold his company."

"He did, huh?"

"And he told me that some guy, King something-or-another, bought it."

"He did, huh?"

"And he said that the guy came from Dallas."

"Yup."

"And he said that he was there today."

"Yup."

"Bently said that he took a liking to you."

"Really? He said all that?" If two people were crafted from the same mold, that would be Ann and Bently. The longer they'd been married, the more alike they got. It was kind of creepy.

"He also said that you got all hot and bothered by him…"

"I did not!"

"And that your dad invited him over for dinner."

"Is there a point to this call?"

"Yes, I'm getting to that." She stopped to take her first deep breath. "So is he there?"

"Who? Bently?"

"No, dummy, the King guy."

"Yup."

Silence. Considerably long for Ann, but the clock only ticked a whole second. "Are you not going to tell me anything?"

"Nope."

"He's there, isn't he?"

"Who?"

"Lily!"

"Fine. Yes." I smiled in spite of it all.

"Right there?"

"Yes. why?"

Another quick silence. "Is he cute?"

I snorted. "Now why should I tell you that?"

"Lily," Momma said loudly from behind me. "You're ignoring your guest."

"Because you'll tell me eventually," Ann said. "And I'm your best friend."

"He's your guest," I shot over my shoulder, and returned to Ann. "That doesn't make you exempt from my refusal to share such information. In fact, you should be grateful that I don't share more of my thoughts with you. We have remained best friends this long for a very good reason."

"So he *is* cute?" she cooed, choosing to ignore my jab.

"Lily," my father tried in his You Listen To Me Right Now, Young Lady voice. "You're being rude again."

"Why don't you come over and find out for yourself," I offered Ann.

"Ooh, really? Can I?"

65

"Lily," Momma said. "You're not a teenager anymore. Get off the phone and be polite to the company."

"No."

Ann asked, "'No' to me, or 'no' to your mom?"

Momma said, "Excuse me, young lady?"

I turned and glared at the three people at the table. Bryce offered up a lopsided grin. "Can't y'all see I'm on the phone?" I said. "Jeesh!"

"You still didn't answer my question," Ann reminded me.

"Listen, I'll take a picture and email it to you. Or better yet, Google him. I'm sure there's a ton of photos out there. He's filthy rich, single and hopefully straight. There'll be pictures." I hit the end button and turned back to my family and "guest."

"Now, was that so hard?" Momma asked kindly. I threw up my hands, left the kitchen and returned a moment later with a digital camera.

"Say 'Cheese,'" I announced and clicked the button. Bryce blinked from the bright flash and rubbed his eyes.

"Lily!" both Momma and Daddy exclaimed. Bryce calmly inquired, "What was that for?"

"For Ann," I said. "She's got the hots for you."

"Do I know this Ann?" Bryce asked.

"I don't know," I shrugged and scrolled through the pictures on the camera, looking for the one I just took. "You look like you're twelve," I told him, presenting the digital image to him.

Bryce didn't even bat an eye at the picture. Instead, he stared at me. "I'm amazed that I only met you a few hours ago, Lily Watson."

"Why, thank you, Mr. King," I said in my best Scarlet O'Hara impression. "I have that effect on people."

"She does," Momma agreed, but without the sarcasm. "Her sister is the same way. Marissa was my beautiful child--"

"Hey!" I declared, "I'm right here!"

"But Lily got the personality," Momma finished. "It's always been a little more *aggressive*." She whispered that last word as though it was dirty. I couldn't believe my ears.

"How can I not be with you two as my parents," I grunted, but Momma continued in her soft voice as though I had never spoken, "Between the two of them, the boys in school never had a chance."

"I guess that explains why I am single."

"You're single because you want to be," Momma pointed out with her fork, and turned back to Bryce. "Marissa was never as picky about boys as Lily. With Marissa, we got a little concerned about her choices in boyfriends. One year, she brought home five different boys. Do you remember that, dear?"

Daddy's face turned a shade of purple. "How could I forget?"

"I'm glad she finally married a good man."

"Yeah, you said the same thing about Nick," I pointed out, "and look how that turned out."

"Now Lily," Momma began, "let's not air out our dirty laundry in front of Mr. King."

I stared at her. God bless her. She was so patient, so

soft-spoken, so calm, but she was also a little slow up the escalator sometimes. "Momma, let me remind you of the strip show you gave *your* guest not ten minutes ago, and the fact that *you* are the one dragging out the family bible and telling a complete stranger all about my childhood."

"Your sister's, too," Bryce added and grinned when I glared at him.

"Lily," Daddy said, finally joining in the conversation. "The world does not revolve around just you."

"Well, Momma seems to think so, since I am constantly the center of her conversations. Next thing I know, both of you will be bitching about how I have yet to give you grandchildren and start pairing me off with the closest, single man."

Bryce stood up so quickly his fork bounced off the table and fell to the floor. "Thank you for dinner, Mrs. Watson. But I should head back to the hotel."

"Oh," Momma keened. "Must you leave so soon?"

"Yes," Bryce answered quickly. "Yes, I must. But I shall see you again in the morning. Lily has invited me to play golf with you."

Momma smiled hopefully, but Daddy frowned, "She did? That was considerate of her."

I snorted.

"If it is an inconvenience…" Bryce said.

"Not at all," Momma said on top of whatever Daddy was going to say. "You can pair with Lily. Bri hates to play, so this will give her time to study her schoolwork."

68

Bryce blinked. "It's the summer," he said with a question in his voice and a little bit of an appalled look on his face.

I filled in the needed information. "We play as three pairs, Momma and Daddy, Marissa and BoBo, me and Bri. Bri is homeschooled and has decided to get out a year early. She has her exam next week."

"Oh, thank you." He actually seemed relieved for the knowledge. And I was sure he'd never met a family quite like mine. His family probably spent their days playing tennis at the country club and sipping mimosa's by the pool, saying things like, "Lovely, darling," in mock English accents and discussing stock portfolios or the next fancy dinner party. Around here, an ice-cold, frothy beer and a mid-afternoon nap in a hammock topped off my weekend.

"Lily, dear. Walk Mr. King out. The night critters have been active lately," Momma told me. Bryce glanced out the nearest window, probably expecting a stampede of raccoons to come through the glass.

"Do I have to?" I whined.

"Yes," the three of them replied. I gave them each a scowl, adding more heat for Bryce's.

"Fine," I huffed. "Come on, Mr. King. We don't want the coons to get you. But if a skunk shows up, you're on your own."

Chapter Six

Lily took her stance at the tee, and Bryce closed his eyes , unable to watch her swing again. After only four holes, Bryce's patience with his ever-growing groin was wearing thin. The woman had no idea what she did to him. Her hips wriggled seductively in those short golf shorts as she sighted her drive and positioned her club behind the ball. Her body flowed like warm molasses as she drew back into the arc with a smooth grace, and he grew a little dizzy, thinking about how that body of hers would move while he cupped her in his arms and kissed her until she went crazy.

Seeing the way she played this game, he could finally understand her view on golf and great sex. If this was her approach to the age-old pairing of couples, then there must be some very satisfied men out there. Bryce hated to think of how many partners she'd had in her lifetime, but he also hated to think that he'd not been one of them.

I've got to get out of here, he thought again for almost the hundredth time that morning. The fresh air and scent of warm pine needles were doing something to his brain. He needed to get back to Dallas, to the glare of glass structures, the hell of heated concrete and asphalt, to the cacophony of honking horns and ringing phones, husbands and wives arguing outside of corner bistros.

This place, this small slice of wooded country seemed as foreign to him as if he'd taken a trip to the outback of Australia. Here, even strangers were addressed as someone might speak to a family member. Just that morning, he'd stopped at a Starbucks for a quick cup of coffee and heard more laughing and joking and off-color, good-natured jabs than he ever thought possible between the five employees behind the counter.

And the main subject of most conversations he'd overheard? Sex. It seemed that clean air and good food was a strong aphrodisiac. Lord knows, Bryce couldn't get it out of his head since he'd been here.

And another stimulant for an active libido? Golf; if watching the other two pairs was any indication. Lily's parents cuddled – if such an innocent term could describe it– in the golf cart when they thought no one was looking. And Marissa and her husband were like horny teenagers on prom night, always touching, and kissing, and going off into the scrub, looking for wayward golf balls. When Marissa hit a line drive on the second hole that landed her ball feet from the green, her husband, BoBo, a tall lanky man with a rather large nose, kissed her with such appreciation and passion, Bryce reddened and turned away. Lily grinned at him and shook her head.

"You okay over there," she yelled across the fairway.

"Fine," he called back and walked down the fairway to get the Watson family out of his sight for a moment.

The whole family played well, and it was obvious that they played often. But Bryce and Lily maintained a considerable lead from the start. He took the first two holes, while Lily scowled at him, with strong drives that left his ball exactly where he wanted it, but Lily's asset was manipulation of the green and her put shot. She had incredible depth perception that kissed her balls into the holes with a deft "plink" each time. She claimed the third hole, smiling victoriously as though to say, *In your face!*

He only smiled in return and congratulated her, as a good partner should. Bryce's turn finished the tee off, and the group set off down the fairway. Their companions traveled in the cart, but Lily preferred to walk, and he accompanied her up to the seventh hole, but she damn near wore him out. His clothes stuck to him, drenched from the summer humidity, and every time he considered riding in the cart, he saw Lily march off down the fairway with her battered, pink bag over her shoulders, and he couldn't bring himself to enjoy that tiny luxury or the couples' open affection in the cart.

"Where did you learn to play?" he asked her as they followed the golf cart.

"In high school. I had a gift," she replied offhandedly, not really bragging, just stating a fact. She was an absolute anomaly. He couldn't get over her lack of vanity. Women liked to talk about themselves, right?

The cart stopped, and her father added, "Lily was All State her junior and senior year in high school. She had a full scholarship to Fayetteville, but gave it up to go to Kansas."

"K State had a better design school," she declared with a little impatience and a look that said, *Leave it alone, Daddy.* They had apparently had this conversation before.

"Lily was as competitive as they come. She could have gone pro," Nomi said, and her sister emphasized in her silky voice, "Yet, she chose to follow her dream and be happy. Such a shame, Momma."

Henry snorted, "If you can call wallowing in mud and sawdust being happy."

"I am happy," Lily claimed petulantly. No one believed her, not even Bryce, but he wisely kept his comments to himself. He was a guest, after all. And sooner or later, he would have to get to the point for this visit. He didn't feel good about that, but he couldn't hang out with the Watsons for too many more days without them getting suspicious or thinking he had a thing for Lily. They would begin planning their wedding and naming their unborn grandchildren.

He really needed to get out of here.

After the round closed and they totaled the scorecard, Bryce didn't have the energy to walk back to the house. He took Marissa's spot in the cart, and Lily walked slowly back to the house with her sister. The one time he glanced back at them, they were deep in conversation, arm and arm. One tall and willowy, floating along the ground with the other, short and muscular. Odd combination of sisters, he thought.

All his life, he'd been attracted to the tall and willowy, but now his eye drew toward Lily, and not because her sister was already married. He watched the way her tanned legs marched with determination through the grass, and the animation of her face as she discussed something sisterly with Marissa. The slightly damp hair of her ponytail was plastered against her neck, and her skin shone with a faint sheen of sweat. She was a lot of fun to watch, that was for sure, but Lily

Watson was a pistol, and he didn't have the time or energy to chase after women like that. Not to mention that she was an employee.

Determined to get the information he came for and go back to Dallas, he decided to ask about her husband and that design software after lunch and forget all about her sexy golf swing and her fascination for playing in the mud.

~~~~~

"Lily, dear," my mother said over a small lunch of tuna salad and iced tea, "Mr. King was telling me that he has never visited Arkansas. Why don't you take the afternoon to show him around?"

I looked at Momma, and then at Bryce. His expression said, "No, thanks," but I beat him to it. "Can't. I'm taking Bri down to the Quapaw Quarter. We're helping with the restoration of the Ledbetter House."

"Can't you cop out for one weekend? Mr. King seems interested in our history. You could show him the Old Mill or take him down to the River Market." Momma added more places to her tour, but I tuned her out and rolled my eyes. Eventually, she wound down and I got a word in.

"Momma, I'm busy this afternoon. I have responsibilities. If Bryce really wants to see our cultural history, he can come down to the Quarter and lend a helping hand." I regretted the invitation as soon as I offered it. After spending the morning looking at that world-class, khaki-encased butt of his and that casual posture with his hands stuffed in his pockets, my endurance not to drool was at its limit. I couldn't be around him for the rest of the afternoon, too.

Bryce noticed. "No, really," he said. "I don't want to be an inconvenience. I should go back to the hotel, get cleaned up, and check in at the office."

I blinked at him. "It's Saturday. What's there to check on?"

"The world of business doesn't stop for a couple words on a calendar," he replied, smiling.

"But a round of golf is a different story," I grunted hotly.

"Exactly," he smiled wider. He left shortly after. And I went out to my truck with Bri in tow.

"I like him," she said, her round face pinched back in her perpetually, sixteen-year-old way.

"Who?"

"Mr. King. I think you like him, too."

I had to admit that I got along with Bri better than my sister did, but today, she was set to annoy the crap out of me. "Nonsense," I said. "He's not my type. He's too rich and too sure of himself."

"That's the best kind."

"And how would you know this? You know a lot of rich and handsome men?"

"Nah, I don't know a lot of anybody. The curse of being homeschooled."

"Good," I said. "That curse will keep you safe."

"Safe from what?"

"Nothing."

"You mean, safe from sex?" She cheeked me with a sly grin.

"Do we have to have this conversation now?"

"Yes, now is as good of a time as any."

I opened my truck door and looked over the hood at her. "I'm your aunt, not your counselor. If you want to discuss sex with anyone, talk to Marissa. She'll kill me for even mentioning it to you."

"You didn't mention it; I did," she pointed out.

"Whatever. Get in. We're late."

"I think you should go for him," she said as I started the engine.

"I don't."

"Why not? Like you said, he's rich and handsome."

"There's more to life than money, Bri," I said as I pulled out of the driveway. "Do other teenage girls talk to adults like this?"

"No, I'm special."

I glanced over and laughed. "Yes, you are."

"So, you'll go for it? I would like a baby cousin soon."

"Oh, no. Not you, too."

"What? What'd I say?"

I turned onto the boulevard and drove toward the interstate and downtown. "Let me set you straight. There is nothing between Mr. King and me. We live in two different worlds. He will not be supplying any baby cousins for you, so get the idea out of your head."

"You know, maybe you should consult him about that. He may have a different opinion."

I didn't comment on that because, frankly, I didn't

want to know what opinions Mr. King had of me. We arrived at the Quapaw Quarter just as Bri pressed a hand to her stomach. "I'm hungry. Could we stop for something to eat? I think I want a doughnut."

My eyes widened. I looked at my watch. One-fifteen. "Shit!"

"Hey, I was only asking."

I parked outside the Ledbetter house and hurriedly dialed Bently's number.

"You're too late," he said, answering the phone with an evil chuckle.

"I got sidetracked. The answer is a doughnut."

"Nope, sorry." I could hear the smile in his voice. "Movie Night, at your place, Wednesday. And I get to choose the movie, and you get to make the snacks. I think I'll want," he paused, rubbing it in, "something Italian."

"Oh God, not *The Godfather* again? I can't stand that movie."

"You don't like *The Godfather*?" Bri asked beside me, and Bently chortled through the line, "And I'm bringing a friend. You'll like him. He's a firefighter. His name is Thomas."

"No."

"Yes," Bently argued. "You know the rules. I get to bring whomever I want, and you can't say anything about it."

"And does this Thomas like *The Godfather*, too?"

"He does a great Brando impression," Bently laughed, enjoying himself too much at my expense.

"This may be the end of a beautiful friendship," I

sneered into my phone and ended the call.

"What's wrong with *The Godfather*?" Bri asked.

"Just get out of the truck."

Chapter Seven

Bryce lay against the headboard of the hotel bed, attempting without success to ignore the ache in his muscles. His shower only added to the exhaustion. *She barely broke a sweat,* he mused. Up and down the fairways, Lily marched. Swinging her clubs with fluid motions of an accomplished athlete. And he played well, too, one stroke under hers, but it took all his concentration to do that.

Concentration he couldn't afford. The memory of Lily's petite body going through the motions of her game saturated his thoughts. No movement wasted, no hit unplanned and each one well executed. And she did it all with a furious passion that left him swollen for more.

I've got to get out of here.

Those words were starting to become a mantra to him. Another few hours in her presence would destroy his reserve. He didn't touch her once during the morning game, but his fingers itched, and he couldn't figure out why. He was glad he turned down her offer to work on a restoration with her, and pissed that he wished he hadn't. He stretched his sore arms over to the phone and called Justin.

"Any news?"

"Nope. Garcia is still missing, and all his copyrights to the designs similar to Ms. Watson's were misfiled. It's taking a little longer to sort out. Some dates are from before the marriage, which we would have no right to, and others are from during the marriage, which Ms.

Watson should have received in the divorce. I haven't found any copyrights from after the marriage. I'm still looking into whether he breached copyright laws, or if he actually designed these houses himself before the marriage and it's all a big coincidence, or if Ms. Watson stole them. It would be easier if you would just ask her to look at Garcia's plans and see if she's got the copyrights to them."

"I'm still working on that," Bryce muttered, rubbing his throbbing shoulder.

Justin paused. "Are you sick?"

"No…"

"Are the Watson's being difficult?"

"No…" Bryce frowned at the receiver. "Why do you ask?"

"Well, this is not like you. I thought you would fly down, ask the questions, get the documents we need, and come home. You sure are taking your time. What have you been doing for two days?"

Bryce wanted to smile, but it hurt too much. "Playing golf."

Another pause. "I'm sorry? You were doing what again?"

"Playing golf with the Watson's."

"Is this one of your suave business tactics? Because we're on a timeline here. If that company is involved in fraud, we need to stop that housing development." Justin's usually rushed manner slowed considerably, and he added, "Does this have something to do with a certain female designer?"

"No," Bryce lied.

"You're lying. I can always tell."

"And how's that?"

"You croak."

Bryce sat up, wincing. "I beg your pardon?"

"You're voice croaks, like you need to clear your throat."

"Good to know," Bryce muttered and added louder and clearer, "Find Garcia."

"I'm working on it. But I also have some bad news. Benjamin Morrissey found out you left town. He hopped the first flight out of Oklahoma City, and has been meeting with the other shareholders all morning."

Bryce chewed on the inside of his mouth. "He didn't waste any time, did he?"

"And he won't stop until he destroys you," Justin added. "He's not just after the company. He wants your head."

Bryce rubbed his temples. A headache, magnified by his exhaustion, pounded out a rapid tattoo onto his skull. He knew that his sexual ramblings would catch up with him one day and take a chunk out of his rear. However, he'd have never guessed that a woman would have died because of his carelessness. "That happened three years ago," Bryce said to Justin. "I wasn't at fault for his wife's death."

"Tell that to Morrissey. He blames you for his marital problems and Charlotte's suicide. And he'll take down the company to get to you. You need to get your ass in gear, get those papers, and get back here before your shareholders revolt. So, what exactly are you doing about all that?"

Bryce sighed heavily and hauled his stiff body off the bed. "I'm helping with a restoration."

"I beg your pardon?" His friend's words sounded oddly familiar. Bryce truly smiled this time.

"I have a date with a certain female designer. We're helping to restore some rundown, decrepit house."

Justin breathed into the phone. "Are you sure you're not sick? I can still schedule that tetanus shot."

"Just find Garcia. And schedule a shareholder meeting for early next month. We'll deal with Morrissey then. I'll call again tomorrow."

"So you are staying another night."

"Looks that way," Bryce said as he put a hand to his back and stretched.

"Well, don't say I didn't warn you."

"Warn me about what?"

"You know how those country women are. Seduce you with those Daisy Duke looks, and the next thing you know, you're flying home with her, pregnant and barefoot." Justin laughed, but Bryce didn't think he was funny.

"Lily is not a Daisy," he snapped at his friend.

"Does she wear shorts?"

Bryce's vision filled with Lily's golf shorts - short enough to barely cover the curve of her bottom without giving him a peek of extra flesh. "Well, yes," he admitted.

"She's a Daisy."

Bryce hung up and changed, annoyed with his friend. He didn't like to be annoyed with Justin. He asked for directions to the Ledbetter house at the front desk, and drove the few blocks. A huge, Queen Ann-style home loomed in front of him. Workers milled around the outside, painting the intricate trim and hauling antique doors out of the house to an area where more people worked to strip away the old varnish and apply fresh coats. He stopped the first person he came to and asked for Lily Watson. The teenage boy pointed to the second story.

Bryce looked up and saw Lily hanging from a harness with a paintbrush in her hand. His chest tightened, seeing her dangling thirty feet from the ground. The boy cupped his paint-smeared hands around his mouth and shouted, "Lil Lil! You've got a visitor!"

She heard her name and twisted around. The harness swung wildly and she bounced against the siding. She looked back at the house and the paint she'd smudged, and cursed loudly, kicking her feet in a mini tantrum. Then she glared down at him. "What are you doing here?"

He motioned for her to come down. He was not shouting up at her with all these people around. She threw up her hands, but, a moment later, she descended to an open window and disappeared inside. Bryce stood on the lawn waiting for her. Dark red paint splatters covered her face and hair, and the side of her hip that had hit the house had a large blotch of paint.

"I can't seem to get any work done when you are around," she grumped as she stomped down the porch steps. "What do you want now?"

Her fierce glare took him back a step, but he fell into

the crystal blue of her eyes and asked the first question that came to mind, "Are you a Daisy?"

"What are you talking about? Who's Daisy?"

"Never mind," he said, shaking away the sudden dizziness. "I've come to help."

She blinked at him, smoothing the hair back from her face, and burst into laughter. Nearby workers stared at them.

"I don't get the joke," Bryce said.

"No joke," Lily said through her mirth. "But let's face the fact. This is not your kind of work, Bryce."

"I beg your pardon?"

"You say that a lot," she commented. "I'm just saying that you won't be able to keep up. This is physical labor. Look at you. One round of golf – and not even eighteen holes – and you're nearly falling over from exhaustion. I'm afraid if you really want to do some good - since your passing out on the front lawn will only get in the way of real progress - you can pull out your checkbook and write a fat donation. We can definitely use the money." She turned and flipped him a wave over her shoulder. "The Association director is over there. In the suit. You two should have something in common."

Bryce glanced to where she pointed. An elderly gentleman stood in the shade of a large oak tree, going through some papers in a binder and talking animatedly into a cell phone at the same time. The man looked like he hadn't held his own baby bottle, much less swung a hammer or swiped a paintbrush.

He ignored the director and followed Lily into the

house. He swept up the staircase behind her, his aching muscles protesting, and stopped inside one of the upper rooms as a young boy helped to hook up her harness. Then she swung out the window again.

"Danny! What'd you do with my paint?" she shouted from outside. The teenage boy shouldered Bryce aside.

"Excuse me," the boy said and handed a bucket out to Lily. The boy pulled his head in the window, looking a little green and swaying against the windowsill.

"Are you okay?"

"He's afraid of heights," a girl's voice answered from behind him. Bryce turned to see Bri standing in the doorway. She eyed him curiously, through that typical rebellious sneer of a teenager. She had her father's lanky tallness, but, thankfully, not his nose.

"I am not," Danny protested as he rushed out of the room with his hand over his mouth. Bri shook her head.

"Good afternoon, Bri," Bryce said politely.

She snorted, sounding a lot like her aunt. "Don't bother wasting your manners on us simple folk. We're allergic."

"Why do I get the feeling you spend more time with your aunt than with your mother?"

"Because it's true," she admitted. "Marissa's great, but she's always on my case. Lily's more laid back. I like her. She should have been my step-mother."

"Don't tell me you got the evil step-mother?" He didn't want to believe that. From the little time he spent around Marissa that morning, she was charming and soft-spoken like her mother; a softer, gentler, taller version of Lily. Not as intriguing as Lily, but a lot nicer.

"Nah," Bri exclaimed. "Lily's the evil one. That's why I like her."

That's kind of why he liked Lily, too. But then he remembered how Justin described her as a cougar, and that she might be capable of replicating her ex-husband's designs for her own use. "Evil how?"

"Nothing serious," Bri brushed off the fierceness of his question. "She's just got a big mouth, and a golf swing from hell. I hear you almost beat her score today. That wouldn't have been good. Isn't that right, Lily?"

Bryce turned back to the window to see Lily peering through it. "Stop telling the truth about me," she barked. "It's embarrassing. Where's Danny?"

"Probably throwing up again," the girl answered.

"Ugh!" Lily exclaimed, throwing her hands wide and making her body swing wide from the force. "Then you have to help me in, Bri. Richie Rich here sidetracked me, and I should be on the back wall."

"No can do," Bri said with a grin. "I'm supposed to be downstairs, painting the kitchen as it is. Ask your boyfriend to help you."

Bryce opened his mouth to refute that, but Bri was gone. Lily let out a huff. He faced her, not quite sure how to help her into the house, but the anxiety of seeing her suspended in the air moved his sore arms out to grab her. He wrapped his hands around her waist and pulled her through the window. She hit her head on the opening, crying out with a loud, "Ow! Watch it!"

"Sorry," he mumbled as he set her on her feet. Her body was a lot softer than it looked. She fit perfectly

86

against him, molding around his planes and angles as though she'd been made just for him. His hands tightened on her hips, drawing her closer to him. She bit her lip and smiled sweetly up at him. That caught his attention. Lily sweet was a dangerous thing.

"Bryce, you can let me go now."

He'd pulled her close and she was pressed against his chest, the heat of her sun-drenched body warming him. The blue in her eyes was brighter, lighter today, but her pupils were so dilated that only a thin ring of crystal azure captured his stare. Without considering the repercussions, he bent down and kissed her.

For a second, she responded urgently, her lips soft and warm and sweet and full, and kissing him back like she'd been thirsting for this kiss for as long as he had. But then a searing pain lanced up his foot as she stomped on him, and when he drew back with a grunt, her palm smacked into his cheek. The echo of her slap reverberated through the empty room.

"I don't like being manhandled," she growled, shoving out of his embrace.

"My apologies, Ms. Watson," he said coolly rubbing the sting from his cheek. "It won't happen again."

She unbuckled the harness, letting it drop to the floor. "Don't get ahead of yourself, *Mr. King*. We don't want you breaking promises."

He backed into the center of the room, giving her the space she wanted and hating every inch between them. "I keep all my promises, *Ms. Watson*."

"And you don't fire indiscriminately," she shot at him from the crystals of her eyes.

"I would ask what you mean by that, but—"

"No need," she cut him short, "I'll tell you. If this is a plan to fire me because I'm trying to 'seduce the boss,' then you are clearly mistaken. I know men like you, and if you throw one fraternization charge against me, I'll take you for everything you've got. The newspapers would love that story."

"I think you've got this all wrong," he tried again.

She didn't listen. She picked up her harness, turned her back and left the room. He had no choice but to follow her. Toward the back of the house, he found her stepping into the straps again and hooking up to another line. She gave him one "go to hell" look, hopped onto the windowsill and swung her legs out, vanishing into thin air.

"Lily," he called, poking his head out. "I came to help you. And that's what I intend to do."

She avoided looking at him as she replied, "Your help has been refused. Go back to your hotel, find some willing, lonely woman to satisfy your needs, and leave me alone."

"Damn it, woman!" Bryce surprised himself. He never cursed, considering it an improper way to express one's emotions. But now, the words fit. He started to add more choice words, but a frazzled woman hurried into the room.

"Oh, good, you're here," she said looking at him. "Here, put this on. I didn't think we'd ever get the back finished today. Lord knows, Lily can't do it by herself." She fitted a similar harness around his waist and legs, overlooking his sputtering protests. "Don't worry.

You'll be fine. It's very safe. You won't fall. And Lily can guide you. She's been doing this for a long time."

Before he knew it, he hung next to an astonished Lily with a paintbrush shoved in his hands.

"Don't talk to me," she said. "Just paint."

By five o'clock, new aches and pains smothered the morning's soreness, but he kept his groans to himself. Lily worked diligently next to him without a single protest to the torturous constriction of the harness, so he wasn't about to display that weakness in himself. The trim on the back side of the house was newly painted and shining, and Bryce discovered a new appreciation for the flamboyant scroll-work that defined a Queen Anne home. The work had been tedious, and, as Lily persistently told him not to paint the brick, or under-siding of the eaves, or the window dormers, or her, the mental stress of doing it correctly adding to his fatigue.

Lily popped through the open window behind him, looking refreshed and not as though she had spent the entire day out in the blistering sun. Bryce immediately jerked upright and refrained from rubbing his aches and afflictions, since he didn't have enough hands to soothe his entire body anyway. Right now he could go for a hot shower and a two-hour massage.

"You look awful," Lily commented.

"Thank you," he replied stiffly.

She shook her head with a tiny smile, and he couldn't help it. "What now?"

"You," she answered. "You surprised me, that's all. You were obviously in a lot of pain, but you never said anything about it."

He gave her a half laugh. "I'll admit. You were right. I'm not used to manual labor."

"You call that manual labor?" She shook her head again. "Really, Bryce. You should get out of the office more."

"So we're back to first names?"

She sighed, but didn't reply to that. Instead, she offered, "Come on. I'll buy you dinner. You at least deserve that."

She bounded down the stairwell with more energy than he could wrap his head around. He trailed after her a lot more slowly, suppressing the wince that threatened to escape with every step. Outside, Lily stood off to one side with Bri, and he heard the younger girl ask, "Danny wants to go over to Kendra's. Is that okay? Can I drop you off and borrow your truck?"

"Sure, but call Marissa first."

"Do I have to?" the girl whined in a voice that resembled Lily's in a creepy, chilling kind of way. Bryce smiled. Those two truly spent too much time together. He rubbed a kink in his neck and noticed that the Association's director still hovered under the oak tree. Bryce walked awkwardly over to him and introduced himself.

"Hello, I'm Bryce King. I understand I can make a donation to your foundation."

The man took his hand and shook it firmly. "John Greer," the man said. "And yes, any donation is welcome. It takes a lot of work to restore these old homes, but we are proud of our heritage."

Bryce pulled out a card. "'A lot of work' doesn't do

it justice," he chuckled wryly. "Have one of your staff send the information to my secretary. I'll make sure she sends a check to the Association later this week."

"Thank you, Mr. King," Mr. Greer said, studying the card. "I appreciate your help. I noticed that you helped Ms. Watson with the upper levels. It takes a steady man to keep up with her."

Bryce liked the man, despite his soft exterior. *Did I really come across like that?* "Yes, Ms. Watson is exhausting," he agreed. "She is some kind of lady."

"You have no idea," the man answered, smiling in a friendly way, as though the two men had been buddies for a very long time. Bryce noticed that a lot of people in this rural state smiled that way. It was heartening...and a little unnerving.

Lily waited for him by his car. "I'm driving," she said as he limped over to her, holding out her hands for the keys. Not a problem. Operating the number of muscles it took to drive a car was a bit past his abilities right now.

"I need to get cleaned up before we go out," he mentioned, relinquishing the keys to her.

"We're not going out," she replied with an even face. "I'll drop you off at your hotel for a quick shower while I grab some take-out, and then we're having dinner at my place." She opened the car door and slid easily into the seat, adjusting it to fit her small frame.

Bryce gingerly lowered his body into the passenger side. "I don't want to be the one that brings up bad memories, but didn't you tell me to leave you alone? Having dinner at your place is not exactly following that command."

"Don't worry," she said smoothly. "There won't be a repeat of this afternoon."

Not particularly pleased with that idea, but also not looking forward to being beaten again, he shut up and she drove.

Chapter Eight

An hour later, Lily parked his rented Mercedes outside a large, English-style cottage with a shingled roof and a gingerbread façade. "You built this?" he asked, recalling what she'd said in her father's office building yesterday, right before she stomped out in a snit.

"Sort of," she said, getting out of the car. "The general structure was already here, but it was pretty run down when I bought it. The roof sagged and most of the windows were broken, not to mention all the termite and water damage. I restored the original house and street view and then added a few extra rooms to the back."

"What is its worth?"

She turned her cool eyes on him. "Do you always look at the world through dollar signs?"

"I have an eye for value," he said calmly. She shrugged, "I paid a little over a hundred for it, but now it's worth four times that."

She grabbed the take-out bags from the backseat and walked up to the front door, a bright red wooden portal with a stained glass, half-moon window above it.

Four hundred percent increase in value? No wonder she couldn't afford it. "How much did you mortgage it for?" he asked, following her inside - and stopped. The front room exploded with comfortable, yet crazy colors, surrounded by white plastered walls, beamed ceilings and gleaming hardwood floors. The interior's focal point was a massive couch in a wild, floral green pattern, topped off with several different kinds of pillows and anchored with a fuzzy, off-white shag rug. The room contained only a few furnishings; drawing attention to two bookshelves built directly into the wall and loaded down with more books than Bryce had hairs on his head.

The house was a far cry from his Spanish-style adobe with its airy rooms and neutral, calming colors. Lily tossed her messenger bag on the floor and disappeared into another room off the living area. He hesitated to follow her, fearing what he might find in there.

"The original one-twenty-three," she answered his previous question. "I sunk in that much in renovations, but I was able to get a grant for most of it."

"How did you do that?" He looked around the polished interior of a normal-looking dining room. He breathed a sigh of relief. The wood surfaces gleamed from a recent oiling, and the furniture was old, mismatched, and comfortable; a perfect fit for this style of home and completely different from the couch and demented pillows. He wondered what her bedroom looked like, and then quickly erased that thought. What did it matter? He'd never get a chance to see it.

"From my work with the historical foundations here in town. I added my home to the list, and with both the entry and the hours of volunteer work, I was able to secure enough." She left him in the dining room to go into the kitchen.

"Just how many hours of volunteer work do you have, Lily?"

"I've put in about thirty a month over the last ten

years, minus a few years worth for when I went to college." She poked her head around a corner and frowned at him. "Why do you ask?"

He did the mental calculations. Thirty times twelve times ten. That's over three and a half thousand hours. No wonder she exhausted him.

He voiced that opinion, and she flashed a smile at him. "I like to stay busy," was all she said.

"No kidding. What do you do for fun?"

"I play golf," she rolled her eyes at him as she returned with serving spoons and plates.

"You tackle golf like another job. What do you do to relax?

"I read."

That wasn't the answer he expected. "You read?" Well, duh...those books out there weren't for decoration.

She faced him with her hands on her hips. "Yes. I read. Us simple country folk can read."

He smiled. "Okay. What do you read?"

"Are you always this nosy?"

"You've already asked me that."

She bit her lip, and he got the urge to kiss away the pain she might have felt. "So I did," she mused. "And I like to read whatever falls into my hands. Mysteries, dramas, biographies, whatever."

"Not romances?"

She slapped her hands on the table. "Listen, if you are just here to insult me, you can leave."

He put up his palms, "I'm just asking."

She exhaled heavily. "I also like to watch movies, go

to art shows, shop at flea markets, and eat. Speaking of which, I'm hungry, and you must be starving."

He ignored her attempt to point out his physical state and continued the inquisition. "Don't you have any friends?"

"Yes!" The sharpness of her tone brought a grin to his face. "I have friends!" she declared as she opened the container of chicken-fried steak strips. "I have a *lot* of friends. I have a *ton* of friends. I spend so much time with my friends that I'm never home. Does that satisfy you?"

He glanced around again. "Just one more question," he said and waited for another uproar so he could watch her skin flush prettily and her eyes glint with annoyance. "Where'd you get that god-awful couch?"

She threw a steak strip at him, and then muttered, "Speak of the devil," when her cell phone jingled that *Little Orphan Annie* tune. Snatching it out of her back pocket, she growled into it, "Hello, Ann." Bryce sat in a ladder-back chair and listened to her speak, still fascinated with the vitality in her face even after twenty-four hours. "I'm psychic," Lily groaned. "Yes…No…Absolutely not…*Ann*…" Then she slapped the two halves of the phone together and announced, "Ann's coming over."

"You don't sound happy about that. I thought she was a friend."

"Not tonight, she isn't," she said and set about dishing out their dinner, adding an extra plate for her "friend."

Bryce wondered if he should just call it a night and

go back to the hotel.

~~~~~

Kill me now, I thought as Ann leaned on the doorbell for a full five seconds and then came on in without permission. Her bright orange, curly head popped through the arched doorway from the living room a heartbeat before the rest of her, her brown eyes widening at the sight of Bryce sitting comfortably at my dining table.

"Hi, you must be Bryce King," she exclaimed, a skip in her step and a laugh in her voice. Too much sugar, that was her problem. "Lil Lil has been telling me about you."

"I have not," I declared and sighed as she shook with excitement. "Sit down Ann. You're bouncing off the walls as it is."

Ann slid into a chair next to Bryce, never taking her eyes, or her smile, off him. Bryce returned the gaze warily. "Pleasure to meet you, Ann," he said smoothly.

"Ooh, handsome and polite," Ann cooed.

"Thank you," he uttered. "I'm afraid Lily has neglected to mention much about you."

"Not to worry," my best friend replied. "I'm here now. You can ask me anything."

"Ann," I warned her, but Bryce gave her a genuine, and mischievous, smile.

"Actually, I was wondering about one thing, and I'm glad you brought it to my attention."

Ann leaned closer on her elbows, pushing her plate

away, her dark eyes glowing like dollops of rich chocolate. "Ask away."

"Why does everyone call her 'Lil Lil'?"

Ann giggled and scooted toward him before I yanked her back into her chair. "That's none of your business, Bryce," I said hotly, getting annoyed and irritated at both of them. This was *my* house. I could kick them both out.

My friend pried my fingers off her elbow and answered anyway. "She has this thing about her height. She's short, you know."

"No," Bryce smiled more. "I never noticed." I shot him a ferocious glare and kicked Ann under the table.

"Ouch," she yelped. "What was that for?"

"Shut up, Ann."

Ann faced Bryce and grinned, "You see? She has that Napoleon complex. Of course, anyone who knows her never notices her height anymore. She's so large in personality. Lil Lil is short for Little Lily."

"Ah, now that makes perfect sense," Bryce chuckled. This time, my aim was at a different leg. I saw him grimace and knew I hit my mark. He raised his eyebrows at me, and I showed him my teeth.

"So, tell me," Ann scooted in her chair to him again. "Bently says you're rich."

"Bently?"

"Her husband," I supplied. "So don't get all worked up with the flirting. She does that to everyone."

Ann kept on going, "I did what Lil Lil said, and Googled you. You *are* rich. And a lot more handsome in person. I want to know what you're doing here in

Podunk country?"

"Business," he answered calmly, but I didn't miss the slight narrowing of his eyes. He was hiding something, and it had something to do with Daddy's company.

Ann leaned over and propped her chin on her hand. "So, Mr. King, are you married? Do you have children?"

"Shouldn't you know the answer to that already? You did say you Googled me." The corners of his mouth tipped up in a half smile, and he offered me an amused glance, not afraid of Ann's boldness. She managed to run off more men that came to my place than my big, green couch did. One look at that sucker, and they begin to wonder if all my screws were tightened down.

"I know," my friend gushed, "but you have such a sexy voice. I love hearing you talk." She edged closer to him. He nearly fell out of his chair trying to get away from her. This time, I intervened a little more physically.

Snatching her by her ear, I hauled her body into another chair and occupied hers.

"Thank you," Bryce murmured quietly.

"Oh, phooey, Lil Lil. You're such a stick in the mud."

"And you were throwing your very married self at my guest," I shot back with a threatening finger under her nose. "Move one inch closer and I'll call Bently."

"Ah, the tigress protects her cub," Ann cooed, grinning with a glint in her dark eyes.

Bryce cleared his throat. "I beg your pardon? Cub?"

I patted his hand. "She's kidding. You're a strong,

virile male with a mind of his own."

His eyes darkened viciously, angered by my sarcasm, and I felt ashamed of myself. He didn't deserve it.

Ann hopped out her chair. "Well, I've got what I came for."

"And exactly what is that?" I asked, ignoring the tense way Bryce's hand had escaped mine.

"To see your new boyfriend," she said with innocence, and then she grinned and was gone. I closed my eyes and breathed deeply.

"Why does everyone assume I'm your boyfriend?" *Wow, what an irritated tone.* The words sounded as though he was spitting them from between clenched teeth. But it was the question itself that caught me.

My eyes flew open and narrowed, "Who else is assuming?"

"Your niece - she said something to that affect earlier."

"Oh, right. Why on earth would everyone think that?"

Bryce shook his head, his eyes still glittering dangerously. "I have no idea. It's not like we put out any signs to suggest it. We can't stand each other." He picked up his fork and dove into the food on his plate with a vengeance.

"I'm sorry," I said simply.

"What for?"

"For that 'virile male' comment. It was rude of me to patronize you like that. I have a big mouth and difficulty keeping it closed sometimes."

He nodded once at me, accepting my apology, but

the dark fever still lingered in his eyes and jaw. I watched him eat. Gracious, that man had an appetite. It was like he'd never been fed before. "Is that why you can't stand me?" I asked.

"I beg your pardon?"

"Okay, stop saying that. It's getting annoying."

"Saying what?"

"Never mind. You didn't answer my question." I folded my arms on the table and wanted to glare at him, but my guilt was still there.

"Aren't you going to eat?" He eyed the untouched plate in front of me.

"Still not an answer." But I took a bite of the country potatoes and chewed. "You said you couldn't stand me. I want to know what's wrong with me. I am likeable - most of the time."

"Yes, you are. Most of the time," he agreed. "But we argue more than anything, and we've only known each other two days. I can't say that's a good start to a healthy friendship."

"Why would we be friends?" I asked. He was confusing me. And I'm never confused.

"Exactly."

I shut my eyes and breathed. "There you go, talking in riddles again."

The sound of his fork clattering on his plate startled me. "Listen, Lily. You are a likeable person, and actually a lot of fun to just watch...

"What does *that* mean?"

"...But just talking to you wears me out. Once I finish my business here, I'll go back to my world, and you will stay in yours. And, with any luck, we will never have to see each other again. So you are right, why should we become friends?"

"Okay. I'll bite," I said. "What is your business here?"

He studied me for a moment, indecision marring the plains of his brow. "My associate came across an irregularity in your father's company."

"What kind of irregularity?"

"The designs for the homes you are building. We think that the company might be involved in fraud."

~~~~~

He studied her face for any sign of guilt. She sucked in a sharp breath. "Fraud?"

"Yes. We have discovered that another architect, Nicholas Garcia, is claiming the rights to some of your plans, and, given the copy of your divorce papers in our possession, we need to know if these particular plans are part of the assets you acquired in the settlement or if they were designed before the marriage and you are the copyright holder. Otherwise, we think he might have had access to your software program." He watched her face transform from confusion to realization to fury.

"Nick," she spat. "That lying, scum sucking, sack of shit! I *knew* he stole my designs. I'll kill him!"

Bryce drew back from the pure hatred in her voice and eyes. He had seen her angry – one, unwanted kiss will do it - but not like this. Justin was right; she was a cougar. But acidic mouth and ridiculing comments aside, he sensed there was good cause for her vicious attitude. That ex-husband of hers must have been a real bastard to trigger such red-hot emotions in such a small woman. She marched over to the wall phone and pounded out a number. A few seconds later, she shrieked and hung up.

"His phone's disconnected! I swear, if I get my hands on you, Nick…" Her eyes darted wildly around the room, and settled on Bryce. She blinked and the anger was gone. "I'm sorry. He makes me so mad sometimes."

Bryce spoke, "Justin is having trouble contacting your ex-husband. Do you know where we can find him?"

"Not now," she commented wryly and dropped into her chair. She put her head in her hands. Bryce studied her. This was a side he had not seen so far. She looked so defeated. He wanted to say something, but every sentence sounded hollow in his mind.

She tilted her face up. "Why didn't you ask about this yesterday? I would have shown you all my copyrights and given you copies of every plan designed on the software and the name of the person who designed it."

"You can do that?"

"Of course, I can," she said, annoyed at him again. "I'm not stupid. I keep a backup of all the plans, finished or otherwise. If you'd only said something earlier, you could be gone by now."

He should have asked yesterday. Instead, he stuck around, watched her fascinating face, played a torturous round of golf with her, fed on the best home-cooked meal in the last decade, painted a three-story house, and stole a kiss in between all that. After seeing Lily Watson dripping mud in her father's office and looking at him with those mesmerizing ice-blue eyes, a part of him wanted to spend as much frustrating time with her as he could. But every time she uttered a sound, she was complaining, scolding, yelling, mocking, or apologizing for the rest of it. And in truth, he kept coming around because he knew he wanted to hear one thing that was nice, or civil, or sexy escape her mouth. But that goal had long-term commitment written all over it. There was only so much Lily Watson he could stand to be around in one day.

I've got to get out of here.

He dropped his napkin next to his plate and stood up. "Since you have all the documents, my business is complete. I'll need you to send everything relevant to this issue to my office. I'll make sure that the originals are kept safe and returned to you when we are finished looking into the matter."

She frowned. "But you own the originals now, Bryce. Shouldn't you keep them?"

He looked at her. She sat so small in her chair, like a little paint-splattered China doll, and he wished he could kiss her one last time before he left. "I may own them now, Lily, but they are your creations. Thank you for dinner. And it was a pleasure to meet you and your family."

Back at the hotel, the soreness in his muscles overtook him, and he fell asleep on top of the bed without undressing.

~~~~~

A persistent ringing jolted him out of his sleep. He cast a bleary glance at the clock. It was four in the morning.

"This better be good," he said into the phone.

"Not really," Justin said. "I've found Garcia."

~~~~~

Three hundred miles away in Dallas, Justin stood in the Dallas County coroner's office, staring at the body of Nicolas Garcia.

Chapter Nine

I hunkered over the strongest cup of coffee my little maker could brew, fighting the yawns that cracked my jaw and made my eyes water. A night of hardly any sleep would do that to anyone. Thoughts of Nick's betrayal and Bryce's retreat infiltrated my sleepless night. Not even a soaking bath in the early morning hours soothed my irritation and relaxed my body enough to drift off to needed dreamland.

I really screwed up last night; that was for sure. I hadn't been around a man that I didn't work with in so long, I forgot how to stroke their egos. I just wasn't that kind of woman. If he asked, I was going to tell him the truth. And I expected the same, even if the question was, "Does this make my butt look big?" I want to know that. After all, how could I fix it if I didn't know?

See, that was what I didn't understand in other women. They gripe and complain about their big butts or small breasts or squishy waists, but they don't want to hear about it, or work towards fixing it. My only physical issue was that I short and square. But that was genetics, and I couldn't change any of it. I didn't have to be happy about it, but I accepted it.

A gentle smile came to my lips as I remembered Bryce telling Ann that he didn't notice how short I was. Either he was a really great liar, or he really did mean that. I'd take either reason at this point, since I couldn't do anything about it anyway.

I should have made more of an effort to apologize for my behavior last night. But he'd kissed me and confused me, and I slapped him for it, when I just wished he'd kiss me again because I hadn't been kissed that way, that spontaneously, since my first date in high school. Then I go and insult him with that 'virile male' comment, and then he was gone. I would never see him again. Now, I only had to think about what I would do with my share of money from the sale of Daddy's company, find a new job, and locate my jackass of an ex-husband. Even after all these years, Nick still found ways to screw up my life.

A soft knock came from the front door, and I shoved my weary self toward it, only stumbling a few times. "It's 6:30 in the morning. This better be good," I said, opening the door. Bryce leaned against the doorjamb with a tired smirk.

"That's what I said at four this morning."

"Great minds think alike," I muttered, surprised to see him. I waved him inside, anyway and staggered back to the kitchen. "Coffee?"

"God, yes."

"I thought you would be packed up and headed home by now." I poured a cup and set it in front of him. He dropped into a chair, cradled the mug in his hands, inhaled the steam, and sighed blissfully as he took a small sip. Then he put the mug down and looked at me.

I pulled the panels of my robe closer together; consciously aware of the sheer nightgown I wore under it. I may live in jeans and t-shirts during the day, but the nighttime was for the wicked. Give me a sexy pair of silky pajamas to sleep in, and I was a happy camper.

"Lily, I've got some bad news."

"Unless, you've come to tell me my wayward ex has croaked, I'm not up to it." I sank down to my arms, resting my head against them on the small kitchen table. Did everyone seem to believe I was glutton for punishment? Even at this time of the morning he looked great, and casual, and so sure of himself that I wanted to strangle him. He was still here, and I would have to get that apology out.

"Funny you should put it that way…."

My eyes truly opened for the first time that morning and peeked at him from under the loose tendrils of hair that fell in my face. He watched me curiously. A funny, grave feeling settled in my stomach. Bryce's own wary eyes were filled with sadness and so much regret that I swallowed and said, "Oh no. He's dead, isn't he?"

Bryce nodded, never taking his eyes off me.

The room began to spin. *Nick.* "How? When?"

"He drowned. The coroner said it happened last week sometime. He was found in the lake by his house, tangled up in some kind of old fencing. A fisherman found him."

I stared at Bryce, getting dizzier. Nick was dead? Lying, cheating, scum of the earth Nick was gone? I felt awful for cursing his memory, but Nick only had himself to blame for my lack of grief. His treachery in the past had created the cynical Lily of the present. However, he was dead, and I hated myself for not feeling more terrible about that.

I blinked to keep the room in focus, but that hurt my eyes, and my throat felt oddly dry and my stomach oddly heavy. Bryce scooted out of the chair and came around the table. The next moment, I was crushed in a hug and tears spilled over on my cheek.

"Lily, I'm sorry. I know you were mad at him, but he didn't deserve this," Bryce whispered in my hair. His hands rubbed my back over the thin robe. His touch felt good. Better than any Nick ever gave me. And another flood of guilt washed over me. I shuddered and wept in his arms, and he held me. It was nice to be soothed, even by a stranger. I thought about the short months I had been married to Nick, and how he never held me this tenderly, not even on our wedding night. I cried harder, and Bryce rocked me, whispering comforting, nonsensical words against my hair. I clenched him around his waist, buried my face into his chest and just cried out the buildup of guilt and sorrow and fear and annoyance.

Finally, I dried up. He tilted my chin. "Are you okay?"

"Oh, no. I got your shirt wet," I moaned, trying to wipe away the blotch of moisture. He pressed his hand over my fingers and chuckled.

"I'll be fine. How are you?"

Nick is dead, I'm not all that sorry about it, and my boss is holding me in his arms. How would you feel?

"I'm okay now." I stepped out of the circle of warmth and regretted it immediately. Fresh tears flowed out, so I hung my head on his chest and the warmth surrounded me again.

"Oh Lily. I'm so sorry. Is there anything I can do?"

Yes, hold me tighter so I can forget all this for just a few minutes. I didn't voice that thought, but it threatened to escape. I sighed, wiping my cheeks. "Really, I'm okay."

"No, you're not," he argued. "You look exhausted. Did you get any sleep last night?"

The lie came smoothly, "Yes." And then I amended it: "A little." I offered a small smile, but the effort faltered when I saw his eyes darken. He bent as though to kiss me again, but stopped short and repeated a previous question.

"Is there *anything* I can do?"

My stunned silence must have answered the question because he drew in a deep breath and dropped his arms, letting me go. "I apologize. That was tactless of me."

He moved to the far corner of the room and crossed his arms across his chest. "I'm flying back to Dallas this afternoon. You may accompany me if you wish. We have been unable to contact any of Mr. Garcia's family. The coroner asked if you could come and identify the body."

"He has a half-sister in Washington, I think," I said, gaining control of my emotions again. "But I've never met her. I don't even know her name."

"Then you will join me?"

I nodded and sat down. There was too much to think about right now. My anger at Nick, my near-remorse at his death, my jumbled emotions concerning the man in my house, my confusion at the look in his eyes as he was about to kiss me…

"What time is the flight?"

"Two o'clock. I can pick you up at noon."

"Okay," I nodded again.

"You should try to get some sleep before then," he advised. This time, I shook my head.

"I can't. I need to pack, arrange a hotel room, call my family…"

"I'll call your family, and you can stay with me."

My head shot up, and he laughed without any warmth to it. "I have a guest house, Lily. I use it for all my visitors. It's barely on the same property."

"No, Bryce. It's not appropriate and I don't want to bother you. I'll call a hotel."

"It's no bother," he firmed, "and I have a very motherly, very protective housekeeper that lives with me. And I'll be a perfect gentleman, I promise you. For all we know, we won't see each other much at all. I spend my days at the office, and you'll be busy arranging Garcia's funeral. Just say you'll stay in my guest house, and then I won't worry about you."

I didn't have the energy to fight about it, or think about why he'd be so worried about me in the first place, so I agreed. He left to go back to his hotel, and I went upstairs to bed.

~~~~~

Bryce turned off the car's engine and smiled at Lily. She had fallen asleep during the drive to his home. He suspected that she didn't get that nap he'd ordered in the morning, and the rest of the day was spent in airports, on a plane that was rerouted to San Antonio, evading news reporters – thanks to Morrissey gaining wind of Garcia's death and the relationship to King

Enterprises – and then the episode in the coroner's office must have sapped the rest of her energy. Dark circles smudged her cheeks and her pouty lips looked on the pale side. She'd refused to eat all afternoon, and barely said a word unless it was forced out of her.

But until they entered the county morgue, her spine remained ramrod straight and her eyes stubbornly firm.

Seeing the bloated body of Nicolas Garcia nearly consumed every ounce of that stiff composure. She sagged against him and covered her mouth to contain the racking sobs. He told the accompanying detectives that she would give a statement in the morning and brought her out to his car and drove her back to his house.

She murmured into his chest as he lifted her out of the car. She was such a little thing, weighing hardly anything at all, and he carried her through the portico and into the house. His housekeeper, Maria, rushed down the spiral staircase as he kicked the front door closed.

"Oh, dear," Maria cried out. "The poor thing. Come. I've got the East Room ready." Maria ushered him up to the second floor, and the previous aches and tenderness in his muscles and joints screamed at him. "In here," Maria whispered, as though he didn't know the rooms of his own house. "On the bed." Bryce set her gently down on the gold-colored four-poster bed, brushing the hair away from her cheek, wanting to pull the ponytail loose and run his fingers through those dark strands of silk. Maria shooed him away. "I'll take it from here. You look terrible. Go to bed."

For a second, he considered the attitude of his employees. They took too much liberty sometimes. But that came with seeing the person, rather than the asset. He looked back at Lily one last time before retiring to his own room, which, he noticed, was on the far side of the mansion.

Maria, Maria, Maria. What did you think I would do? Seduce a sleeping, mourning woman? He shook his head and fell into bed, fully clothed and wincing from the torture of bouncing on the mattress, his body yelling at him to be still and to stop moving around so much.

He woke the next morning feeling like he had been drugged.

Rolling to the side, he squinted at the time, and sat up quickly. He had slept through the whole morning. On a Monday. Usually, he made a habit of arriving at the office by seven, before anyone else except Gloria, who was always sitting at her desk when he walked through the outer door. Once, he even tried to slither in at five o'clock, but she was there, giving him a Mona Lisa smile. He suspected that Maria had called Gloria after he left, but he had never been able to prove that.

Bryce showered and dressed hurriedly and raced across the upper landing to Lily's room. It was empty. He went down the back stairs to the kitchen. Laughter and clinks of breakfast dishes being served met him. Lily's bare legs poked out from under the kitchen sink. Justin sat at the small kitchen table with Maria, talking to the woman plumber as though they had known her their entire lives.

"Justin," Lily's voice called out. "Hand me the pipe

wrench."

Justin got up to dig through the toolbox next to her. "Um, a what wrench?"

Her sigh echoed through the kitchen, and Bryce heard her mumble something about rich men and dots, and he smiled because Justin wouldn't understand her annoyance even if he pointed it out to him. "The one with a red handle. It looks like a bent pair of scissors with teeth." She arched her fingers to make the shape of the tool.

Justin placed it in her hands, grinning triumphantly at his correct guess. Maria snickered. They didn't notice him, so he leaned against the wall and watched how her tanned legs wiggled further into the dark opening. Justin told her about the time he went with Bryce to Japan on a business trip, describing how Bryce continuously knocked his head on the doorways, and how he almost ended up engaged to the daughter of one of his patrons while there. Not a memory Bryce was proud of.

Lily laughed out loud and then cursed. She jiggled free of the sink, sucking her thumb between a humored grin. The chatter died down as her eyes met his. "There you are," Maria said, waving him over. "Sit and eat. I called Gloria and told her that you won't be in today."

"Aha!" he exclaimed, wagging his finger at her. "I knew you've been talking to Gloria about me."

"Nonsense," the woman sniffed. "You're not that interesting."

"Who's Gloria?" Lily asked, standing up with a twinkle in her eye. She piled the tools into the box.

"My secretary, and the bane of my existence," Bryce

answered haughtily. He eased into a seat. "What are you doing?"

"Maria said she had a leak."

Maria nodded, "I told you about that last week."

"Why didn't you call a plumber?" He kept his eyes on Lily. She bent over to heft the toolbox in her arms, and he admired the curve of her bottom and hips. He also noticed that Justin's jaw slackened. If his friend had been close enough, he would have punched him.

"I called one," Maria explained. "But the leak came back. Lily looked at it and said that some kind of valve thingy was loose."

Lily frowned and shook her head. "Your plumber probably left it loose on purpose. That way, you would have to call him back to fix it, and you would have had to pay a full hour's worth of work for only ten minutes of repair. It's a classic con. You shouldn't use him anymore."

"I won't." Maria smiled graciously at Lily. "Thank you. It's nice to have someone who knows these things." His housekeeper astutely chose not to look in Bryce's direction, but Justin did. He laughed in Bryce's face and popped him on the shoulder.

"How are you this morning?" Bryce redirected the conversation.

A momentarily sadness coated Lily's smile, but she waved it away. "I'm fine. Thank you for everything, but you really should have taken me to your guest house."

"Honey, if he had done that, he would have a lot to answer for," Maria declared from the stove. She scooped pancakes onto a plate and dropped them on the table in front of him. "I might have spanked him."

Bryce frowned at the older woman, but Lily giggled and the sound was so lovely and rejuvenating, he forgot his ire. He caught Justin's eye. His friend jerked his head toward Lily and smiled. *Keep this one*, the look said.

Bryce shook his head and ate. Justin hadn't seen her snits yet. He might change his mind.

After breakfast, Lily wandered outside to admire the pool. Justin clicked his tongue and said, "Nice girl."

"You're married," he reminded him.

"But you are not."

"Nor do I intend to be anytime soon."

"She's a lot prettier in person and not as short as I thought," Justin continued. His usual rushed behavior was muted, and Bryce narrowed his eyes at his friend.

"What are you up to?"

"Nothing," he flashed a grin. A little pause that deepened Bryce's suspicion, and Justin added, "Startling eyes. What color would you call that?"

"Blue."

"No, doesn't quite describe them. They're almost like,well,like…"

"Crystals?"

"Exactly," Justin grinned again. "And with a face like that, she looks like a, I don't know…."

"A china doll?" Bryce offered.

"Yes," Justin patted him on the back. "Exactly. I bet she's an athlete of some sort. With legs like that…"

"She plays golf."

"Oh, really? Is she any good?" Justin arched an eyebrow.

"She has a handicap of ten and a half."

Justin chortled, but before he could spill out any more prolific musings, Bryce informed him. "She also likes to read, watch movies, go to flea markets, and play in the mud. Anything else you need to know, Cupid?"

"Nope, I think you've about covered it."

"Good," Bryce said as he went out the back door.

Lily sat on the edge of the pool, dangling her feet in the water. He smiled to himself. Careful not to startle her, and cause her to fall into another body of water, he approached loudly and settled next to her on the concrete. She twitched her lips and wiped sweat from her brow.

"Did I tell you I hate Texas? You have no trees here."

"We have trees."

"No, the shrubs that you call trees do not count. I miss Arkansas's trees. The pines can grow so thick that not a single ray of sun can filter through." She flicked her toes, splashing water back at them.

"If you wish, you may swim. There are some suits in the bathhouse. I'm sure you can find one to fit."

"Really, Bryce. I don't want to be a bother. I need to go down to the police station anyway. Do you think Maria will call me a cab?" Lily pushed herself up and gazed down at him. In one fluid motion, he stood.

"I'll drive you, or you can use one of the cars in the garage."

She blinked at him, biting her lip. "You're being really nice. What happened to arguing all the time?"

"Since you are the one who usually initiates our

fights, you should ask yourself that."

"Right." She walked away, but stopped after a few steps. "I'll borrow a car, if that's okay."

"The keys are on hooks in the garage. Help yourself. Are you sure you want to go alone?"

"I'll be fine."

Chapter Ten

I took a deep breath and got out of the red sports car that I'd borrowed from Bryce. My choice of vehicles in his garage also included a black Suburban and a rusty old Jeep, both of which appealed to me for different reasons, but the temptation to mold my body against the soft, supple leather seats of the Porsche was too much to ignore. And it smelled like him, too.

The drive into the city was pure torture.

The Dallas police station loomed in front of me, and I dreaded the questions that would be asked. The morning had started awkwardly. Waking up in Bryce's home – not his guest house - had been an awkward start to the morning. Maria's motherly concern had gone a long way to easing my anxiety and making me feel better.

And meeting Justin was a plus. Too bad he was already married. He matched my energy. Not that Bryce was lazy or anything, but he sweated the small stuff, like painting a hundred year old house while it seemed like Justin just might be able to keep up.

Maria and Justin made it worthwhile to be up. They chatted easily with me, treating me as an equal and not as some country hillbilly. Not that Bryce was snobby or talked down to me, but his twelve-point-whatever millions were too much to comprehend. We were just too different.

"Can I help you?" the woman at the front desk asked when I finally reached the front of the line.

"I'm Lily Watson. I'm supposed to see Detective

Johnson about the Garcia case." She checked a clipboard and directed me to a waiting room. Half an hour later, a policeman called me back, scanning my body with a metal detector and digging through my handbag. He took any suspicious items, held them up to his eyes, and after sealing them in an envelope, handed over a ticket for retrieval. I sighed. What was the world coming to when the police didn't trust you?

"Ms. Watson," an aging, gray-haired man greeted me. "Thank you for coming by today. I know you must have a lot to do today. Please follow me."

Three hours later, the questioning began to resemble an interrogation. Maybe if I hadn't been so sarcastic and aggravated by their insinuations, I wouldn't have been answering the same questions over and over. I had myself to blame, really...

"Do you know of anyone who would want to kill your ex-husband?"

"Only everyone he ever met," I scowled at the man.

"Including you?"

I gazed at him evenly. "Yes. He lied to me, cheated on me, stole from my father, stole from me, and he was a lazy son of a bitch, to boot."

Detective Johnson ignored my scornful words with obvious patience. "Where were you last week between Monday night and Wednesday morning?"

"At home, in Little Rock, three hundred miles away, doing my job and living my life." I slumped back into the hard metal chair, rubbing my neck. This was getting tiresome. These were the same questions asked in different words, and I was at the end of my rope.

"What did he lie to you about?"

"He told me he was from Iowa."

"And that was a lie?"

"Yes, I found out he was from Oklahoma City, born and raised."

Detective Johnson scribbled in his notepad. Already, he was on what seemed like his thousandth page, but his hand never ceased to tire. "And what did he steal from you?"

"He stole blueprints of a house design I was working on."

More note taking. I elaborated, "I had to submit a modified design to gain the copyright, but he has the original designs. Or rather, *had* the originals. They were the basic designs for a software program I was working on."

"And from your father? What was stolen from him?"

"Money," I snapped. The detective looked up at me with that "calm down, young lady" look. I huffed at him and crossed my arms.

"How much money?"

"Twenty thousand. We got it back before he could use it."

He flipped through an open file folder. "There is no mention to theft charges on Nicolas Garcia."

"We didn't press charges. I wanted a divorce. He signed the papers without dispute in return for his freedom."

He gave me another look, this time it said, "not very smart," but I stared at the ceiling and huffed again. He leaned back in his own chair and dropped his pen to the pad. "Can you tell me where your father was between Monday night and Wednesday morning?"

I had another short answer to spit out, but my memory stopped me. Daddy was here…in Dallas…signing the company over to Bryce and supposedly visiting Aunt Gracie in her retirement home.

"Ms. Watson? Please answer the question."

Daddy wouldn't, would he? No. I mentally shook my head. He didn't like Nick. He wouldn't seek him out for any reason. But the dilemma with the blueprints and the computer program rang in my head. If Daddy thought that Nick had reason to stop the sale of the company….no. Daddy wasn't a violent man. He never even spanked me as a child.

"Ms. Watson? Is there anything you want to tell me?"

I looked at the man. "Am I under arrest?"

His eyes tightened. "No, you are not."

"Then I suggest that if you have any questions for my father, you ask him. I'm done here." I stood up. He didn't stop me from leaving, and I retrieved my belongings from the front desk, heading out into the smothering Dallas sun.

I just fueled the detective's skepticism, but I didn't care. I needed to call Daddy and ask him a few questions myself. Something just wasn't right. If Daddy went to see Nick, he'd tell me, right?

Yeah, just like he told me he was selling the company.

I walked toward Bryce's car, frowning down at my feet and not really watching where I was going. The owner of that sports car leaned against the hood, all casual-like, and he reached out to steady me as I stepped off the sidewalk and stumbled in the gutter. Despite myself, I grinned when I saw him. The sun dripped off his russet hair, and he wore the same sunglasses from the first time I ever laid eyes on the man. Only today, he wore a buttery yellow golf shirt and a pair of dark denim jeans.

"How can you stand there like that? This heat is killing me," I said, looking up at him and shading my eyes with my hand.

"The heat is bearable. It's that Arkansas humidity that's a killer," he smiled.

"Why are you here? I told you I'd be fine."

He shrugged. "I got worried. I've been trying to call you for hours."

That brought back all my scorn for the law enforcement department behind me. "I was being difficult. They don't like that in there."

He smirked. "I imagine not. Did the detective give you any trouble?"

"Nope. I'll not answer that."

He was in the process of opening the passenger door for me and stopped. "Is this about expensive golf clubs again?"

"No, this is about you buying off cops to ease your discomfort," I replied. "I'll say something about how I came out of there feeling like I just sat through six hours of inquisition, and you'll get all vigilante on me and start shelling out wads of Benjamin's to shut up curious detectives. Next thing you know, I've been blackmailed into fixing your plumbing for the rest of my life because I know too much."

Bryce blinked at me for a second and then laughed. "I'm not a criminal," he said and opened the door. "But the plumbing part, that was interesting. If that was a sexual innuendo, I'm growing quite fond of your humor."

"I'm not that complicated," I answered with a flash of my teeth. "If I was talking about becoming your sex slave, then I would have said that."

After he lowered into the driver's side, he turned to me, "If I didn't know any better, I'd swear you were flirting with me."

"If I didn't know any better, I'd swear you were, too," I spit, snearing. "But as it is, the subject is moot."

"That's a shame," he smirked at me as he started the engine and drove away from the police department.

I was curious to know how he'd appeared beside his Porsche, out of thin air. I turned to ask him, but he looked so very sexy just sitting there that I decided the world of Bryce King held a lot of mysteries that I didn't want to know about. Instead, I asked a different question, "Where are we going?" He directed the car south, not north where his huge, massive, enormous golden mansion sat on top of a large chunk of prime real estate.

"I promised my sister that I would drop in when I got home. You don't mind, do you?"

"No. I guess not. It's not like I have a choice, do I?"

He shot me a sidewise look and then maneuvered over to the shoulder of the divided highway, twisting in the seat to face me. "You always have a choice. Would you like me to take you home? I can visit Lisa tomorrow."

His piercing gaze held me, and I noticed how tiny the inside of the car really was. There wasn't enough air inside to avoid inhaling his spicy scent. He rested an arm over the back of my seat as he waited for my reply. Without any warning, he flipped my ponytail. "Do you ever wear your hair down?"

"It's hot when it's down."

"Then cut it."

"But I like it long. It makes me look like a girl."

He threw back his head and hooted loudly. "It's not really funny," I complained. "I'm built like a linebacker. I'd like to have one thing that is unquestionably feminine."

He choked back the rest of his amusement and turned to me, "Trust me, Lily, no one would ever consider you as anything but a girl."

I shoved my arms under my breasts in annoyance. "Laugh it up. I know what I look like. I'm short and thick. My hair and what little I have up front are the only things that tell others I don't have an extra part hanging from my groin."

He scanned my body. I shifted under the intense scrutiny. Then he bowed close to me, capturing my gaze with his. "Lily, I am not gay—"

"I caught that pretty quickly" I retorted.

He smiled softly. "Then this would be considered an attraction to the opposite sex."

I furrowed my brow, not understanding, but he

clarified as he managed to move around the impeding stick shift and latch his lips to mine. The hand that toyed with my hair, secured my head from retreating.

Oh Lord! It was like that first kiss all over again. My knees turned to jelly and my heart skipped several beats to gain the speed of a racehorse. Back at the Ledbetter house, the rush of my arousal scared me more than his kiss. And I had to practically beat the mess out of him to get him to stop. My reputation would never recover if someone found me ripping the clothes off my boss in public.

But we weren't in public now. Granted, we were parked illegally on a Dallas highway with a stream of traffic zooming past us; however, those curious eyes of passers-by only spied our fraternizing for a fraction of a second.

I clenched my fingers together to hold them away from his clothes. The kiss lasted only a few agonizing, brief seconds. Bryce withdrew, breathing heavily on my mouth. "No, Lily. You are definitely a woman."

"Good to know," I said, proud of the clarity of my voice. He sighed and pulled out into traffic. I turned to stare out my window so he couldn't see me licking the taste of him off my lips.

A little later, he eased off the highway and meandered down a winding road to a lakeside community. Stopping in front of a cedar-log two-story cabin, we got out of the car just as the front door opened, and, like they'd stepped out of a clown car, a trail of little boys ran out to greet us.

"Uncle Bryce," one boy exclaimed, crawling up his

leg. Bryce laughed and picked up three of the boys in both arms.

"Lily, these are Benji, Julian, and Aaron." He introduced them, pointing to each with his chin. "Those guys, I have no idea who they are." He nodded at the other two, and one of them giggled and said,

"We live over there," and pointed across the street.

"Oh, okay. Come on in, Lily, and meet the baby, Lenny. And Lisa, my sister."

"There's another one?"

Bryce hauled his wiggling load into the cabin. His sister, a slender woman still battling her pregnancy weight and bearing the same reddish-brown hair as her brother, met them inside.

"Lisa, this is Lily Watson. Lily, my sister, Lisa."

"Nice to meet you," I said, offering my hand. She carried baby Lenny on her hip and was covered in some sort of chocolate mess.

"Oh, it's a pleasure, Lily," Lisa said to her, waving away the handshake. "Sorry, I'm a mess. In fact the whole house is a mess." She directed a glare at her brother. "Thank you for bringing guests over without calling ahead first."

Bryce dropped his cargo and grinned. "Don't worry about Lily. She likes dirt. She plays in it all the time."

"Still, you could have warned me."

"Really," I said to her. "Bryce is right. I don't mind. A home is not a home without a little clutter."

The oldest boy placed himself in front of me. "My name is Aaron. You have fourteen buttons on your shirt." Then the boy ran into me, throwing his arms in what must have been a hug of some sort. I stumbled from the force, but he was gone before I could return the favor. I looked at Bryce and Lisa for an explanation, but neither commented, so I let it go.

"Come on back to the kitchen," Lisa said as she hefted her youngest and picked her way through the jumble of toys on the floor. "I'm sorry, but Bryce never mentioned you before. How long have you known each other?"

"Three very long days, two extremely torturous hours," I glanced at my watch, "and twenty-seven excruciating minutes. Give or take a few extra seconds for the initial shock to wear off."

Lisa's jaw dropped. She snapped it back in place and grinned at Bryce, "Oh, I like her."

"I thought you would," he said and lowered down to a stool at the breakfast bar. I joined him.

"Can I get you anything to drink? I have tea or lemonade."

Bryce winced, "Any chance you bought those at the store?"

"No, I didn't. I made them," his sister replied, sticking her tongue out.

"I'll have a beer," he said, and whispered to me, "I suggest the beer."

"Okay…"

Lisa popped the lids of two bottles and placed them on the bar. "Bryce has this fear of home-cooking."

"Only yours, darling."

"So far, no one has died from my cooking."

"That you know of."

"And the kids are healthy as horses," she remarked, as though he didn't say anything. "I don't suppose he has eaten your cooking, Lily? He really does have a fear."

"Actually, I haven't cooked for him. But I can. My mom taught me."

Bryce slithered around on his stool, "Nomi taught you to cook?"

"Um, yeah."

"Are you any good at it?" he asked intently.

I grinned. "No one has died."

He leaned forward, "Can you teach Lisa?"

Lisa slapped the back of his head, resembling my mother in a vaguely comforting way. I laughed at that. "Oh, I like her," I said.

~~~~~

Lisa chuckled behind him for the third time. He ignored her and watched Lily playing with the twins in the backyard. Well, Bryce thought, for anyone else, wielding a hammer and power tools would be considered manual labor. Lily was actually repairing some storm damage to the boys' tree house and showing them how to swing the hammer and not smash their fingers.

"I have to say, Bryce. I'm impressed. You managed to find a woman that did not step right out of the pages of Vogue and has the three dimensional personality to match." Lisa shouldered up next to him, wearily resting her head on his arm.

"We're just friends," he clarified.

"Then I suggest you make your move. Any woman who can do that is a keeper. Lord knows you know absolutely nothing about tools."

"She's not interested. She told me herself."

"But what about you? Are you interested?"

He smirked down at his little sister. "Oh, very, but it's not going to happen. We do nothing but fight, and the woman wears me out. She goes non-stop all day without resting."

"So do you," Lisa informed him. "I've known you to work up until the sun breaks through the morning sky."

"Yeah, but Lily's a little more physical with her work. She climbs all over houses like a spider and digs through dirt and mud for the fun of it. In one day, she beat me at nine holes of golf and then hung suspended from the side of a three-story house, just to paint the trim. And she considers that a light day." He swallowed the rest of his beer and tossed it in the recycling bin.

"That's your third one. Are you driving?"

"Lily can, if it bothers you."

"It bothers me," she said. "So, she beat you at golf, huh? What was that like?"

"Oddly exhilarating," he chuckled. Just then, Benji shot through the back door. "Uncle Bryce, come see what Lily did!"

He followed his nephew out into the yard. Lily's ponytail was draped over the side of the tree house and he gave it a tug. "Ow!"

"Rapunzel, Rapunzel, let down your long hair," he called to her.

She lifted her head over the side and peered down at

him. "Not by the hair of my chinny-chin-chin."

"Wrong fairy tale," Bryce smiled up at her. It felt odd to look up at the woman.

"Right fairy tale," she argued, "You're just playing the wrong part."

"What part should I play?"

She flashed her teeth. "You're not a prince; you're a wolf."

"I thought I was a dot."

"You've been upgraded." Her head vanished and the pounding of hammer to board vibrated through the air.

"What are you doing now? Adding a bathroom? Get down from there. The boys want to come up."

Amazingly, she obeyed, her shapely legs emerging from the trap door. She jumped to the ground. "Bathrooms are very important," she claimed. "They are the selling points of a house."

His nephews shrieked and scampered up the ladder. "Very good, Rapunzel. The locals are happy."

They watched the boys eagerly re-explore their tree house and fly down the zip line and across the grass. Lily giggled with them, and tried the zip line at the encouragement of the boys. Bryce's eyes never left the merry twinkle in her face. The same twinkle from this morning laughing with Maria and Justin.

A huge lump of jealousy settled in his chest. She never looked at him that way. No, she was always picking fights with him. The noticeable difference disturbed him. What would it take to get her to smile at him like that?

Aaron, a boy who never opened up to strangers,

babbled nonstop at her heels and even told a joke that made sense. Lily did that. Something about the woman made everything, and everyone around her feel comfortable and special. Her smile lit up her face and infected all within the immediate vicinity. Bryce felt a small twinge around his chest cavity as he watched her interact with his nephews. For a second he allowed himself to imagine a tiny girl with Lily's eyes and smile and his family's reddish hair playing with the boys.

Bryce jolted backward. Where in the blazes did that vision come from? No way. No how. Bryce King refused to gamble with a child's life. A child from his gene pool had the probability of being born autistic. He looked at Aaron. His nephew was happy most days, but Bryce had seen the bad times also. He couldn't take that kind of chance.

"Do my eyes deceive me?" His brother-in-law, David, clapped him on the back. "Emperor King fixing a tree house?"

Lily turned at the question, raising an eyebrow at Bryce. She didn't comment on her involvement in the small project.

"David, this is Lily," he said. "Lily, my brother-in-law."

"Wow, that's some grip," David declared as he shook her hand. Then he turned her palm up, peering at the rough skin. "Bryce, you cheat! She fixed the tree house! I should have known not to go against my better judgment."

"I had to try," he hitched a shoulder with a smirk.

Lily rolled her eyes. "Oh, yes," she agreed. "So far,

I've managed to get him to walk the whole length of a golf course, eat my mother's home-cooking, swing from the roof of a Queen Anne, *and* hold a paintbrush. He's coming along nicely, but tree houses are a little out of his league."

David readjusted his hanging jaw and turned inquiring eyes to Bryce, "You ate someone's cooking?"

Bryce drew himself to his full height. "I did."

David leaned closer and whispered, "Was it any good?"

"My mouth waters just thinking about it."

Lily's expression was blank. "Is she really that bad?"

Two pairs of male eyes turned to her. "Yes," they answered in unison.

"Well, that just won't do." Lily marched up the lawn and into the house. The men followed, a little more hesitantly, but curiosity eventually pulled them into the kitchen.

Lily had Lisa by the shoulders. "Before I leave, you will learn one recipe that won't kill these men." Lisa's eyes were wide and she bobbed her head. Bryce and David settled on the stools, clinked beers together as they wagered a bet, and witnessed the amazing act of Lisa learning to cook.

Chapter 11

"That's it," David remarked, tossing his napkin on his empty plate. "Lily, you are a genius. I could eat your mashed potatoes every night for the rest of my life."

I smiled with gratitude. "Lisa made them. I only directed."

"I don't care," he shook his head. "I'm hiring you as a full time culinary expert. Whatever you want, you can have it."

"Sorry," Bryce chirped up. "She's already under contract. She's mine."

"I'm not anybody's," I noted, although belonging to Bryce sounded dreadfully tempting, "especially yours."

He gave me a wink. "I can double David's offer. Triple it, even."

"I don't want your money," I asserted with a sniff. All talk ceased, and they *stared* at me. "What?" I asked looking at everyone. "What'd I say?"

Lisa and David swiveled their heads to Bryce with identical smiles.

"I'm confused," I said, watching the three of them communicating silently. Finally, Bryce shook his head and said, "Don't be. It's a private joke of Lisa's."

"And I suppose I'm not in the loop?"

Lisa patted my hand, "Really, it's nothing. I've been telling Bryce for years to find a woman who didn't want his money. And it was about time I held a little girl in my arms."

"Oh," I drew out the word. "Huh?"

"Well, it's late," Bryce announced, scooting away

from the table. "We should hit the road."

"Lily's driving," his sister stressed to him. He sighed and nodded.

Back behind the wheel, I followed his directions to the highway and let the silence stew for a while, but the tension inside me bubbled up. "I never used to be confused."

"I beg your pardon?"

I shot him a sidewise glance. "Before I met you, I was never confused. But you and your sister have a talent for talking in riddles. I can't seem to get over it."

"It's nothing personal," he muttered.

"What did she mean about holding a girl? She can't seriously be thinking of having another baby so soon."

Bryce chuckled softly. "No, that isn't what she meant. She was talking about me. Lisa thinks I need to settle down and get married. Start having kids."

"Oh, God," I groaned. "It's a disease, I tell you. Suddenly, everyone has baby syndrome. Momma and Daddy have been giving me grief about grandchildren for years. Bri wants a cousin. Marissa wants a nephew. I swear, if one more person pushes me towards pregnancy, I'm going to just get it all cut out."

Bryce swiveled his head on the headrest. "I promise I won't say one word about you having babies." He crossed his heart. I twitched my lips with a charmed sniff.

"What about you? What's your baby story?"

He fell quiet. I diverted my eyes from the dark road to scan his face. His eyebrows were drawn together with solemn thoughts.

"Did I say something wrong?" I asked.

"No." His reply was oddly quiet. He breathed heavily a few times. "Did you notice something odd about Aaron?"

"Um, well, yeah. I didn't want to say anything, but he has something, doesn't he?"

"Asperger's Syndrome. It's been tough on Lisa and David. That's why I don't want kids."

I risked another glance. His head was turned away, but I could see the reflection of half his face in his window.

"I didn't realize that it was genetic," I said.

"It's never been proven," he said to the window, "but I won't take that chance."

"So, you're just going to adopt?"

He swiveled toward me. "Why would I do that?"

I shrugged. "Don't you want to get married?"

A phantom smile flickered on his lips. "Are you proposing?"

"Heavens, no!" I denied fiercely. "I'm just asking. If you ever get married, what would you say to your wife? 'Honey, don't bother counting your days, because my little guys aren't coming anywhere near you'? Sounds to me that you're being just a bit selfish. But then again, big, bad, rich wolves like you can do whatever the blankity-blank they want."

"The 'blankity-blank'?" Now he smiled fully, looking deliciously handsome, and completely off-limits.

I hitched another shoulder, keeping my eyes on the dark road. "I figured that since you never curse, I'd spare you the corruption for now. Let you fill in your

136

own words."

"So you noticed that, huh?"

"That you don't say curse words to get your point across? Yeah, I noticed. I also noticed that you've changed the subject," I said, pointing a reproachful finger at him.

"It's not a subject I enjoy," he admitted and turned back to his window, rebuilding the wall around himself, and letting me know quite plainly that I could badger all I wanted. He wouldn't rise to the bait.

I drove in silence, hoping I was going in the right direction, since after a while he became eerily quiet. I looked at him again. Relaxed against the headrest, he let his eyelids droop closed. I gave him a rough shake.

"Wake up. I need a navigator to find your castle."

"Just keep on going."

Soon, his quiet snores accompanied the purr of the engine, but I kept going. Eventually, not even the stripes on the road looked familiar. I pulled to the side, and knocked him on the head. "Bryce! I think we're lost."

He shot up, hitting his head on the roof of the car. "Ow! Where are we?"

"That's what I want you to tell me."

He looked around, studying a nearby road sign. "You passed the turn."

"I figured that out a long time ago. How far away are we?"

"About twenty miles."

"Great." I did a u-turn on the empty highway, praying a police cruiser wasn't hiding out somewhere, waiting to catch illegal u-turn makers.

"Why didn't you say something earlier?"

"Because you told me to keep going, and then you fell asleep." I stomped on the clutch and shifted gears with force.

"Easy," he said. "She's a kitten. You have to treat her like one."

"Bryce, I'm tired, I'm lost, and I'm mildly pissed off at the moment. Don't make it worse."

"Sorry, Lily. I'll keep quiet."

"No, don't do that. You'll fall asleep again, and we'll never get back."

"Okay," he said, yawning. "What do you want to talk about?"

I screwed my face into a glower. "What day did Daddy come see you last week?"

"Thursday. Why?"

I chose my words carefully. "The police asked me about his visit."

"Did they say why?"

"They knew that Nick stole some money from him, and they wanted to know where he was when Nick died." I gripped the steering wheel, staring out into the night.

"Do they think your father had anything to do with it?"

"I don't know," I said quietly. "I need to talk to him. I should have called him today."

Bryce sat silently next to me. I peeked at him. If he fell asleep again... "I'm sorry," he finally said. "I shouldn't have dragged you out to Lisa's."

"No, no. I had fun. You have a wonderful family. I like meeting other people's families. It makes me happy to see normality once in a while."

I didn't have to look to sense his mocking grin. "Lily Watson, I do believe that was a compliment."

"What?"

"You just said something nice about someone. I've been waiting for this day since I met you."

Did he mean that as an insult? I almost pouted. "I can be nice."

"And now you've proved it. I'm proud of you." He reached over and patted my hand on the gear shift.

"Oh, I get it," I let out a cynical laugh. "This is payback for that 'virile man' comment. All right, you got me. We're even."

The warm hand disappeared and Bryce sighed, "And she's back."

"Ha, ha."

"Turn here," he directed with a deep chuckle. Even if he wasn't being vindictive, I could have curled up in that rich sound and died from the luxury of such a laugh. I made the turn, and he directed me through the neighborhood streets and into his front circular drive. "Just tell me how to get to the guest house," I said.

"Your belongings are already here, Lily. Come on up. We're both too tired to go any further." He emerged from the car and waited for me to comply.

"It doesn't feel right," I commented. "I should really go stay somewhere else."

"Why?"

Oh, let me see…because I am having impure thoughts about

139

my host, who is also my boss, and sleeping in the same house with him will keep my eyelids open all night?

"It's not appropriate," I gave him the CliffsNotes version of my reason.

Bryce threw his arms wide. "Lily, I live almost a quarter of a mile from the nearest person, and the only other person in the house is Maria."

"Exactly. We're practically alone. It's not appropriate," I repeated, crossing my arms. "We barely know each other."

He stepped closer to me. I stepped back. The Porsche blocked my escape after three steps. "Lily, how old are you?" he asked smoothly.

"Twenty-nine." Why did that matter?

"And I'll assume that since you were once married, that you are not a virgin, correct?"

"Excuse me?"

He continued, "Therefore, you are a consenting adult, experienced in the ways of men and women, and we don't live in the seventeenth century."

I crossed my arms under my breasts and scowled up at him. "Is there a point to this?"

"Absolutely," he uttered in a near purr, his face inches from mine, and his breath heating my cheeks. "One, no one will consider it inappropriate if you stay in one of the spare rooms. Two, it's too late for you to move your things to the guesthouse, just because you are afraid of a little non-existent gossip. And three, since this isn't the seventeenth century, you, my dear, will have to carry your own luggage yourself if you decide to hike the half mile to the guesthouse. I'm tired. I'm going to bed."

With that, he turned on his heels and sauntered through the massive front doors, whistling, of all things. I considered throwing a rock at his retreating back. But instead, I just stood there, taking in that casual walk and that tight rear in those jeans, and I was thankful for the cool night air. After that little upbraiding, he turned me on even more than when he kissed me in car. That night, my fantasy gladiator whistled while he worked me over. And it was mind-blowing.

~~~~~

I woke up late the next morning, yawning contently. The queen-sized bed just sucked the tired out of you and gave me plenty of room to tussle with my gladiator friend. I felt great. Then I thought about Daddy and slumped back into the pillows again. I groaned and called him. He told me the Dallas police already contacted him and asked him to give a statement at the local police station in Little Rock.

"Daddy, did you see Nick while you were here last week?"

His heavy sigh answered my question.

"Yes, I did. I didn't want to upset you. Somehow he found out I was selling the company. I'm not sure what he wanted. He never told me."

"Daddy, the police think you might be involved in his death."

"I received the same impression," he said.

I squeezed my eyes shut and forced out the next question. "Did you?"

Without hesitation, he said, "No, Lily. I didn't. I saw him Monday afternoon, visited Gracie on Tuesday and Wednesday, met with Mr. King on Thursday, and drove home on Friday."

I heaved out a sigh of relief. "Okay, Daddy. I believe you. I knew you weren't capable of hurting anyone, but I just had to hear it from you."

"How are you, Lil Lil?"

"I'm fine. I'm over the shock. I just need to arrange Nick's burial and then I'll come home. Tomorrow or the next day, I'm not sure yet."

"Okay," she heard him say, followed by a muffled sniff. "Make sure you let Mr. King know that you appreciate his hospitality. Sometimes you forget to do that. Vivian once told me about his guesthouse. It's almost a mansion by itself."

I agreed, not having the heart to mention I wasn't staying in the guesthouse, and hung up, parting with, "I love you. Tell Momma, I love her."

Bryce was sitting at the kitchen table when I came downstairs. He held the newspaper to his face and sipped a cup of coffee. He put them both down as I dropped into a chair.

"Sleep well?"

I smiled. "Actually, I did. That bed is heaven."

"So I've been told."

Maria handed me a cup of coffee and asked what I wanted for breakfast. "Oh, I'm not really hungry," I said. Bryce grunted a warning.

"You better eat," he said. "Maria takes her duties very seriously. She will follow you around all day until you do eat."

My eyes met Maria's. She stuck her fists on her hips, and her gaze confirmed Bryce's announcement. "Okay, then some toast or yogurt, if you have any."

She placed both in front of me. "Shouldn't you be at work?" I asked Bryce.

"I'm working from home today," he answered. "What are your plans?"

I took a bite of toast. "I have to go by the funeral home and make arrangements. After that, I need to call the airport and book a flight home, I guess."

Bryce snapped the newspaper up to cover his face. "Already done."

"What? Which part?"

"Both," he said from behind his shield. "You can call the funeral home and change anything you wish, but it's been taken care of."

"And the flight home?" I asked sharply. Maria barked a small chuckle behind me.

"It leaves tomorrow at eleven o'clock."

"Why not today, since I obviously don't have anything else to do?"

The corner of the paper tipped down to reveal his raised eyebrows. "Because you deserve a break. Relax. Enjoy yourself. Go for a swim. Take out your aggravation on the driving range. Do whatever you want. Go shopping if you wish." The paper shield went back up, and his coffee cup disappeared behind it as well.

143

Maria refilled my cup. "Is he always like this?" I asked her.

"I don't know, dear," she said. "I haven't seen this much of him since I started working here. I'm not sure if that's a good thing yet. He's starting to annoy me, too."

The sound of a gurgled choke emerged from the other side of the paper. Bryce dropped the paper and wiped his mouth with a napkin, glaring at us. We grinned back.

"You have a driving range?" I changed the subject.

"Out past the tennis court, near the guest house. It's only a one-man range, but there is a clubhouse."

"Good enough for me. You got clubs, too?"

"Do I have clubs?"

He pushed away from the table and hauled me to my feet. He led me through the rear of the house into a room I had yet to see. "Choose," he said, waving his arm into the space. Rows of racks lined the walls, and hundreds of clubs – drivers, irons, woods, putters, wedges, and hybrids – of every type, style, and brand filled the racks. A few empty bags stood in one corner, but a battered bag of a well-used, older set of clubs leaned against the wall closest to the door.

"Whose are these?" I asked, touching the cracked, leather bag.

"Those are mine," he said. "You can't have those. Choose something else."

I drew out his driver. "A Callaway. How old is this?"

"Almost twenty years," he replied. "It was a birthday gift."

I admired the simple design, and a new appreciation for Bryce hit me. He didn't need to hide behind fancy equipment. "Which birthday?"

"My sixteenth."

"You're thirty-six?"

"Thirty-five," he corrected me. "My birthday is in November."

I dropped the club into its bag with regret and faced the fearsome racks. Taking my time, I chose a driver that surged through my swing with ease and some other clubs that fit my size and felt comfortable in my grip. Bryce hefted his own bag and a box of balls.

"I thought you had to work."

"The perk of a home office," he grinned and led the way outside.

The driving range might have only allowed one person to swing at a time, but the accompanying amenities could have supplied an army. The tee mat sat under an enclosure that had been built for the golfer's comfort. Ceiling fans, a wet bar, a sitting area with wicker couches, and an adjoining clubhouse were all included. Not to mention that the nearest golf course was only a cart ride away, over a paved path that led out his back gate.

Bryce set his bag to the side and fed the golf balls into an automatic ball dispenser. I looked out over the range. The yardage signs gleamed like new and the Bermuda grass layered the ground like a thick carpet. It was the nicest driving range I had ever laid eyes on. To be wealthy and white collar... "Do you ever use this?"

"At least once a week. Justin uses it more than me,

but he has an evil slice and needs all the practice he can get. Ladies first," he waved me over.

After the first drive sent my ball to the two-fifty mark, a thought hit me. "Uh, Bryce? How do you get your balls back?"

I peeked over my shoulder for his answer. He had a funny smile and was shaking his head, laughing to himself. "What?" I asked.

"Nothing. Just a wayward thought."

"Well? How do you get your balls back?"

He let out another laugh, but replied, "I hire some of the caddies from my club to come by twice a week. They collect the balls, mow the grass, keep the place in good shape."

I took a few more swings then stepped aside to allow him his turn. I was still having difficulty wrapping my head around him. He was a millionaire, drove a red Porsche, hired people to pick up after him, and lived in a house the size of Rhode Island. But Bryce King was not the man I assumed him to be when we first met.

He was on a first-name basis with all of his employees; he played with twenty-year-old clubs; he talked to me as an equal when he wasn't drawing out a snobby "I beg your pardon;" he played with his nephews as roughly as any overgrown kid; and he obviously enjoyed kissing me, a concept I was still having trouble comprehending. And still, none of that mattered. I was going home tomorrow, and, like he said, with any luck, we would never see each other again. It was for the best.

He whipped his driver again and again with those

fluid, relaxed motions, sending his ball closer and closer to the three-hundred mark. The muscles in his arms, back, and shoulders rippled through the cotton of his shirt, and a lock of hair fell over his brow when he sighted his ball. He was unquestionably sexy. And decidedly out of my league.

I let out a rueful sigh.

"Something wrong, Lily?"

I looked up and met his stare. "No, nothing's wrong."

"Your turn." He moved behind the bar and set a bottle of water on the counter for me. Then he reclined on one of the couches to wait and watch. After a few minutes and only six swings on my part, he cleared his throat and hurriedly stood up.

"I need to check on some things for work," he said. "Feel free to stay out here as long as you wish. There are more balls in the clubhouse." He turned on his heel and left, practically sprinting away from me.

How very cajoling.

Well, it was for the best. I felt exposed with him watching my every move. Still, his absence bothered me. My swings became lazy and less accurate as the morning progressed. Eventually, without him there to egg me on, I grew bored.

Oh God! Did I just think that?

Golf bored me? That's it! I have to leave here. That man was changing everything I thought I knew myself. I liked being the cynical, crabby sister who could find peace in the club and green.

Maybe, it was just the heat. A swim would cool me

down. Where did he say that bathhouse was again?

Chapter Twelve

"**M**r. King," Gloria said through the videoconference screen on his computer, "I sent the information from the Quapaw Quarter Association to your accountant. He's here to see you about that."

"Put him on," Bryce said, not looking up from the performance analysis of his company's stock. Ozzi Stern appeared in the digital screen, pushing his coke-bottle glasses up his nose.

"Bryce, I need you to authorize the new charity. I can add it, but our donation budget for the year is already tapped out."

Bryce added some notes to the analysis before giving Ozzi his complete attention. "Hold that thought for a moment. I need you to send someone from your office to Little Rock. I acquired a construction company there, and I want the books looked at."

"Anything in particular?" Ozzi asked, scribbling a reminder in the margins of his papers.

"Look for anything out of the ordinary, mostly concerning employee bonuses, petty cash, or irregular expenses. See if Mr. Watson is doling out advances to his workers off the books. The company is in the red. I want to know how he got there. Get the business information from Gloria."

"Will do," Ozzi said.

"Alright, give me the rundown on the charity budget," Bryce glanced at him. "Let's see where we can cut back."

Ozzi shuffled his papers. "The U.S. Autism and

Asperger Association receives 3.5, the Red Cross and the American Cancer Society both get 1.5, the 61 Foundation and Special Olympics are in the 750 range."

Bryce waved a hand to stop him, "Do we support any local charities?"

Ozzi flipped to the last page. "One. The Covenant House. It receives fifty thousand."

"Double it," Bryce commanded him. "Add the Quapaw Quarter, and match it. Take from the others to balance the budget. *Except* the Asperger Association. We don't touch that one."

Ozzi grinned at him through the computer monitor. "That was my plan as well."

"Then why do you ask me about these things. You're my accountant. If I didn't trust you with our money, you wouldn't work here," Bryce commented with an exasperated tone.

"Because you're the boss, Bryce," Ozzi emphasized and moved out of camera range. Gloria's face popped back into view. "I also have some new contracts for the research department for you to sign and a list of holiday bonuses that you have yet to approve. Mr. Clark from *D Magazine* wants to reschedule his lunch on Thursday for next Monday. Your dentist called, reminding you to make your six month appointment..."

Gloria talked for the next half hour, filling him in all on the work he'd missed over the last few days. He gave her directions that she really didn't need to hear – she already knew what to do – and signed off the videoconference. But now, without the distraction, Lily filled the void.

Down on the range, he had watched her wriggle her hips and attack her drive seductively. After only a few swings, the heat became too much, and the urges harder to ignore.

I should have put her in the guesthouse, he reprimanded himself. If she asked to go there tonight, he would let her. Only this morning, he was half way across the upper landing when Maria caught him and said, "You leave Lily alone. She's still asleep."

He almost went to her room anyway. It was his house! But Maria blocked his path and he went down to breakfast. Then she arrived down the back stairs, dressed in more of those short shorts and a sleeveless top, and her hair in that God-forsaken ponytail. Just once, he would like to see it down.

Maybe I can coax her to dinner tonight. Somewhere nice. She would have to wear a dress.

Bryce, pleased with his decision, forced his brain to concentrate on the work in front of him, and, before too long, the lunch bell rang through the house.

"Has Lily come in?" he asked Maria as he entered the kitchen.

"A while ago. She went swimming to cool off. Lunch will be on the veranda." Maria shouldered him aside as she prepared a tray of sandwiches and fruit. Bryce went out to the pool to check on Lily. He didn't expect to see her half-naked and dripping wet.

Well, of course! She went swimming, after all!

Maria followed him out and hustled him toward the veranda. She called to Lily, who swam to the nearest ladder and climbed out. Bryce realized that if he went blind right that second, he would be happy knowing that the last thing he saw was Lily in a turquoise string bikini with a sheet of wet hair plastered to her back.

He scoured his mind for the suitable phrase to describe Lily's body. Tanned and muscular didn't quite cut it. Eye-popping and mast-raising might have been a bit crude, but add in bewitching and fluid, and the description got a little closer to the actual truth.

She grabbed a towel, wrapped her body in it, and padded over to the covered dining area. "Oh, good. I'm starving." She heaped her plate with food and lifted a sandwich to her mouth, stopping when she noticed he was staring at her.

"Are you going to eat?"

"Where did you get that?"

"Get what?" Her brow crinkled as she made a confused frown.

"That suit," he pointed to the straps emerging out of the towel.

She looked down. "The bathhouse," she said. "You said I could borrow one."

"Did you have to choose that one?"

She dropped the sandwich onto her plate and stood, keeping the towel secured around her chest. The next thing he knew, the bottoms slithered to the ground and the top was untied and pulled out of the towel. "Here," she said, tossing the wet pieces on this lap. "You can have it back. If I knew you would be a hard-ass about what you loan out, I wouldn't have bothered."

She dropped back to her chair, hitched the towel tighter around her breasts and ate her lunch. Her cool, crystal eyes gleamed at him in a challenge. Bryce lifted the soaked swimsuit off of his lap and threw it over his shoulder. He ignored the wet splotch on his pants.

"I'm not being difficult," he indicated. "I only wanted to know why you decided to wear the skimpiest suit you could find."

"It was not skimpy," she insisted. "And besides some grandma-looking one-piece, that one was the only one that fit me. I don't know who usually swims here, but you know a lot of skinny women."

Bryce thought about that. "Yes, I suppose I do. Most of the women I've dated were like supermodels."

Lily snorted in disgust. "Tall, beautiful, and graceful. I've lived in that shadow all my life."

"Yes, they are tall and beautiful, but every one had a cold heart and a greedy nature. And they are *too* skinny. I'm beginning to appreciate a woman with meat on her bones." Bryce popped a grape into his mouth.

"Meat," she snorted again. "I'm not sure you know what to do with a real woman."

"That sounded like a challenge, Lily."

"No challenge," she mumbled around a bite of turkey and cheese. She swallowed, washed it down with a gulp of lemonade, and smirked at him. "It's just an observation. I'm sure you have women falling all over you all the time. Those aren't real women. Real women don't drop into your lap, Bryce. We want a man who respects us and is willing to work at keeping us."

"Is that what you want, Lily?"

"Me?" she squeaked and took another drink. "Yes, I suppose I do. But I also want someone who would never lie to me, never cheat on me, and can keep up with me. I don't have the patience to baby a man and haul his lazy, tired butt after me. I'm an active woman. I need an active man."

She reached across the table to the fruit bowl, and her towel slipped a fraction of an inch. The barest hint of cleavage stared back at him. Lily didn't seem to notice. She reclined against the back of the chair, peeling an orange. The towel slipped another fraction. Bryce felt his corneas ache from the strain, willing the terrycloth barrier to loosen just a little more.

He jerked away from the sight and sighed. "Your towel is falling."

Lily examined her wrap and smiled. "So it is." She hitched it up under her arms and secured it.

"So, you need an active man?" Bryce inquired. "Would you settle for one that was a little less active than you during the day, but promised to wear you out every night?"

She stopped peeling the orange. The corner of her lip curled up as she bit it and considered his question. "I suppose that could work, but I have yet to meet such a man."

He decided to tease her. "So you have slept with every man you've met?"

She smiled and tipped her head, "No, I haven't, as you well know. I'll amend my statement. I have yet to be involved with such a man."

"How many involvements have you had?"

She shook her head as she separated the orange wedges. "Nope. I won't answer that. I believe I once told you that my love life is none of your business."

"And yet, you sit here practically naked, tempting me."

She didn't reply, but she devoured wedge after wedge with an impish grin. And she licked the juice off her fingers as an added bonus.

"All it takes is a little nudity?"

"Nudity is good."

"You are such a man," she snorted.

"Yes, I am," he agreed. They shared an innocent smile, but he had a nagging feeling she wasn't teasing him. She finished her lunch and gathered her dishes.

"Maria will take care of that," he told her.

"Yes, I know. But why should she come all the way out here to gather *my* dirty dishes, when I am going in that direction anyway? A cardinal rule of construction: it takes a town to raise a barn." Her plate clinked on the sandwich platter, and she piled on the fruit bowl and lemonade pitcher, leaving only two fingers to clip onto her glass. But the problem of her towel presented itself. With every movement, it threatened to come untucked, and Bryce, not sure if he could handle even that small strip show, groaned and stood up.

"Give them here. You go get dressed." He waited until she slipped into the bathhouse before piling the dishes onto the large tray that Maria had left on the table. Lily would have tried to carry it all on her own just because she thought she could.

Bryce hefted the tray and took it into the kitchen. Maria stared at him oddly, because Bryce King holding a tray of dirty dishes did not belong in this universe, but she maintained a polite silence, and Bryce ignored her as well. Lily followed him in a few minutes later, her hair pulled up again.

"I'm going to take a shower," she announced.

Bryce cleared his throat, "Lily, would you have dinner with me?"

She stopped at the foot of the stairs. Maria busied herself at the sink. "I've had dinner with you every night for the past five days."

"I know, but there is this really great restaurant called Dakota's that I know you will like..." he trailed off, stuffing his hands in his pockets and waiting.

Lily furrowed her brow. "Okay. That sounds great." She turned and wandered up the stairs. Bryce went back to his office to make the reservation and stare at the wall until dinner.

But one little problem walked through his office door an hour and a half later.

"Kristen," he said, surprised to see her.

"Good evening, Bryce," she returned, unslinging her handbag and sauntering over on very high heels. "I hope you do not mind. I let myself in."

"What do you want?" He almost grimaced. He had never been that crass with a woman before. Except Lily, but she welcomed it.

Kristen's perfectly plucked eyebrows hit her hairline. "I thought we could talk."

"About what?"

She frowned. "Okay, I understand that you are upset with me, but I think we should discuss this as adults."

"And what are we discussing? You said all there was

to say when you walked out."

She reached the edge of his desk and sat down on it, crossing her legs and leaning into a seductive posture. "I was wrong. You were right. Vivian Corter did not have her eyes on you. She eloped this weekend in Las Vegas. Did you know that?"

Bryce leaned back in his desk chair and steepled his fingers in front of his chin. "I knew only of her intention. She asked me to look over a prenuptial agreement, even though I told her I knew very little about them."

"And you did not correct me?"

"You had your mind set on leaving. I've known from the beginning that arguing would not matter."

She eyed him. Her hair was swept back in an elegant bun at the nape of her neck, and she wore a short sundress with a tailored jacket designed to enhance her slender waist and large breasts. There was once a time her figure and presence dried his mouth and made him giddy with need.

Now…how did Lisa put it? She looked like a life-sized Barbie doll, too perfect to be realistic.

When he made no move toward her, she unbuttoned her jacket and slid if off her shoulders. "Bryce, baby, I was wrong," she repeated, cooing. "I miss you. Give me another chance to show you how much you mean to me."

He watched warily as she slid off the polished wood of the desktop and lowered into his lap. Her perfume lay heavily in the air between them, and, with Kristen this close, he could see the makeup that made her skin look flawless at a distance.

Visions of Lily, clean scented and smooth, skin unadorned, skittered through his mind. Bryce cleared his throat. "I'm afraid those days are over, my dear. I've moved on. I've found someone else." He stood, dumping her to the floor. She screeched at him.

"How dare you? No one turns me down."

"There is a first time for everything, Kristen. I suggest you get used to it."

She picked herself up. "Oh, right. I heard about your 'someone else,'" she sneered. "A country bumpkin with pigtails, no less. Really, Bryce, I expected better from you."

"And you were right in your expectations. Lily is a considerable improvement," he countered calmly.

Kristen turned a shade of fuchsia, which did not look so good with her coloring. "*Lily*? Did you take her lollipop as you robbed her cradle, Bryce? How old is she? Sixteen?"

Bryce walked over to the door and waited patiently for Kristen to get the message. She whipped her jacket off the desk and marched from the room, bristling with anger. He nodded at her as she flew by him, but his grin only slipped out when the front door finally slammed behind her. Lisa would be proud of him.

~~~~~

I heard Bryce leave the kitchen after he asked me to dinner, and scurried back down the stairs as fast as I could. "Maria," I hissed, waving her over. "What kind of place is Dakota's?"

"Oh, it's very nice," she said, smiling broadly. "My late husband took me there on our last anniversary."

"What should I wear?" That was a question I rarely asked anyone, but Bryce King just asked *me* on a date. Maybe, not a real date. It didn't mean he had any feelings for me, but I liked him and I didn't want him to be embarrassed by me.

"Well, a dress, I suppose," Maria replied. She watched me chew my lip. I didn't pack any dresses. And I was a mess. Make-up and hairspray were not used on a normal day.

"That might be a problem," I mumbled.

"I'll take care of it, dear. I have a niece that can help you. She's very good at these things. You go take your shower, and I'll call Rosa." She flapped her hands at me.

After my shower, I dressed in some jean shorts and another one of my many t-shirts, this one with Tinker Bell on the front. Maria knocked on the bedroom door and entered with a twenty-something, petite girl who could have been born from a ray of sunshine. Joy, energy, and brilliance of character radiated off her.

"Lily, this is Rosa. Bryce said your reservation is at eight. That should give you enough time."

"Enough time for what?" I asked, wondering what I had just agreed to. "I thought we were just getting a dress."

"Oh no, Miss Lily," Rosa beamed at me. "You dine at Dakota's, yes? We visit my sister's shop. Lorda will do your hair, your nails, toes - the whole enchilada, okay? Come. We go."

"Um, I don't know if I can afford all that," I said to them.

"Don't worry about that, dear," Maria said as she guided me out of the house. She bent down to whisper in my ear, "I'll take it out of the emergency fund."

"I'm not sure if that is an insult or not." But she didn't hear me. Rosa pushed me into her lime green Beetle, and we were gone.

After four hours of shopping, being poked, prodded, painted, rubbed, plucked, and snipped, I didn't feel like me anymore. Heaven knows, I didn't look like me. Rosa chose a stunning halter dress in cornflower blue with all the accessories and a pair of high-heeled sandals to match. "Men like tall women," Rosa remarked as I tried to walk on the strappy stilts. Lorda trimmed my hair and curled it into soft waves that fell down my back, covering up the skin where the dress failed. Then her assistant refurbished my nails and skin until the rough exterior was buffed away and a shiny new me stood in my place.

Rosa dropped me at the mansion a little before seven-thirty. I heard Bryce yelling, "Where the devil is she?" as I rushed through the portico, stumbling on the heels in my haste.

"I'm here," I called, slamming the door behind me. "I'm late. I know. I think Rosa got a little carried away." Bryce stopped on the upper landing when he heard me. He looked down at me, resting his hands on the wrought iron banister, and blinked.

"Oh, Lily dear," Maria gushed, coming forward. "You look beautiful."

"Oh, uh, thank you. Your nieces were really nice. I didn't realize how bad I was until after the third hour in their hands. Lord, I'm tired. And I didn't even do anything!"

Maria complimented me again and again. She took the shopping bags with my old clothes, and I peeked up at Bryce. He still had not moved. "Well? Come on," I shouted at him. "We're going to be late."

He took each step as slowly as possible, his jaw clenched and his dark eyes narrowing. I tapped my foot with impatience. "Cat got your tongue?"

"I just wanted you to wear your hair down," he muttered, shaking his head.

"Is that why you asked me to dinner? So I would let my hair down?"

"Yes," he answered stiffly.

I pursed my lips. *It doesn't matter now*, I reminded myself. "Well, it's down, I'm hungry, and you're driving. Let's go." I looped my arm through his. He wore a dark gray pinstripe suit, and I was happy that the heels allowed me to rise above his chin.

~~~~~

She didn't. Bryce peeked at her again. *She did.*

Lily, or someone vaguely resembling Lily, fidgeted in the passenger seat, tugging down the hem of the short dress, and nervously picked at the pink polish on her new nails. Her long, thick hair was finally cascading down and across her shoulders in gentle waves. But if this "person" were the result of his wish, he'd take the ponytails.

Makeup. He groaned inwardly, and swallowed. She was wearing makeup. And perfume! Oh, hell…and the heels. High, neck-breaking heels. Even her toenails were shiny and painted.

Frustration coalesced in his center. Barbie Doll Lily. He never thought he'd see the day. What was she thinking?

She looked beautiful, he'd admit to that, but she was always beautiful. Just naturally exquisite. Nothing natural about her now, he thought bitterly.

The drive to downtown was excruciating. The sickly sweet scent of her perfume made his eyes water, and every time he turned a corner, her dress hiked a little further up her thigh. Between the sight of her bare legs, crossed demurely, and the rest of her appearance, his body couldn't decide between being pissed-off or turned-on.

Then, of course, as soon as they arrived at the restaurant, Kristen sidled up on the arm of a balding, smug fool. She brushed by with only a cursory glance at him and a sneer for Lily, and entered Dakota's.

Wonderful.

Chapter Thirteen

My fork clanged loudly as I threw it down on my desert dish. "Okay, what's the problem?"

Nearby diners turned their heads at us, and I directed a "Mind your own business" glare at each of them. Bryce sat across from me, stiff as a board. He didn't answer.

"Listen, something is the matter. You've barely said two words to me all evening, and you won't even look at me."

Bryce's eyes darted between my face and my dress, and then settled on some point over my left shoulder.

"Well, then," I announced. "I guess I'm ready to go."

Like magic, a waiter came over. Bryce said a few muted words to him, and then we stood and left the restaurant. Dakota's was a charming place, with waterfalls cascading in the patio that cooled the summer night air, but Bryce's behavior pushed my patience. Despite the eerily quiet drive in his car, I had hoped for a rather nice dinner. I did get all dressed up, after all, but did Bryce say anything about that? No. In fact, the few times he even looked in my direction, the look was so full of wary astonishment and horror that I wished I had just worn my faded jeans and a ratty t-shirt. At least like that, he paid attention to me.

I didn't know what had gotten into him, but obviously I'd overstayed my welcome here. I offered to drive back, since he was laden down with nearly an entire bottle of wine. Halfway there, I dialed the house.

"Maria, it's Lily. I hate asking this of you, but would

you take my things over to the guesthouse tonight?"

There was a momentary pause, and Maria said, "Of course, dear. Is everything alright?"

"Fine. I'm just thinking I would be more comfortable in the guesthouse." I hung up my phone and glanced at Bryce. Still, he kept quiet. A tiny nerve in his cheek pulsed angrily.

What is wrong with him?

But I decided that I just didn't want to know anymore. Up to this point, he had been welcoming and friendly. Something had changed, and I couldn't put a finger on it.

I parked outside the front door. He got out, and disappeared into his steroid-injected adobe. I drove the Porsche into the garage, and walked to the guesthouse. It was a two-story townhouse structure with the same Southwest exterior, but it was still bigger than my own home. Maria had kindly dropped my suitcase and overnight bag in one of the bedrooms; the place had four. I stripped off the dress, hung it up, and took a shower, hoping the hot water would calm my irritated state and help me sleep.

Just after midnight, I was still awake.

I meandered out to the balcony to look at the stars, and to keep my mind off Bryce, but like all aggravating men, he managed to slither back. The clubhouse at the driving range was lit up, and I could see Bryce chopping at balls as though they had murdered his entire family.

I had to be at the cemetery early in the morning to witness Nick's lonely burial, and then go to the airport. This might be the last time I see him, and I had a few things to say.

Approaching the covered veranda of the clubhouse, I belted my robe around my waist and stopped a minute to lean against a post and watch him. It really was too bad he was my boss. With a body like that and the courtesy he showed me over the past few days, he was extremely attractive, and I never wanted a man more than I did right that moment.

He had just become my own worst nightmare. No more blonde idiots for me. No, now only one man stimulated my libido, and I couldn't have him.

The ball dispenser emptied, and he turned. His gaze zeroed in on me.

"I couldn't sleep," I told him. "And since I may never see you again, I wanted to thank you for helping me with Nick and the police and all. You've been very kind, and I appreciate it."

He stuffed his club in his bag. "Why?"

"Well, because you didn't have to do any of it. It's not like we know each other very well, but you've been a friend – except for tonight. I don't know what that's all about, and I guess it's really none of my business anyway, but…"

"No," he shook his head at me. "I meant, why won't we see each other again."

"Oh, that. I have to be at the funeral home early, then to the cemetery to send Nick to the underworld, and then I fly home after that. Home sweet Little Rock, here I come." A slight chill reminded me that I was dressed only in a thin set of short pajamas and a satin nightdress that came well above my knees. I crossed my arms over my chest, hugging back the goose bumps. "Well, that's all I wanted to tell you. Please, tell Maria, 'thank you' for me. Good-bye, Bryce King."

The thick grass of his lawn tickled my toes, and the light from the guesthouse shone at me like a beacon. One more night. Just endure one more night in the immediate vicinity of Bryce King, and then I would be done. I'd go back to my life, forget about his casual stance and his expensive cologne and the way he enjoyed annoying me because he always smiled the quirky little grin when I grumbled at him.

By the time I entered the guesthouse, my shivers were no longer from the cooling night air. I was going to miss him.

"Lily…"

I jumped out of my skin and whirled around. "Oh, jeez! You scared me half to death!"

Bryce stood in the doorway. If he'd knocked, I didn't hear it. I placed a hand over my racing heart and concentrated on getting my breath back.

He came slowly to me. "Lily, I'm sorry. I have been acting peculiar tonight. It's just that I saw someone that I didn't expect—"

"Bryce, you don't owe me any explanations. You can afford to be eccentric and a little loony at times. It doesn't matter. I saw that woman that kept shooting evil eyes at us, but it's not my business. I don't need to know—"

"I'm upset with you," he admitted in a rush.

I nodded slowly. "Yes, I figured that you were. I'm sure you were embarrassed with me—"

"Lily, stop—"

"No, I overstayed my welcome. Don't worry. I'll call a cab and be out of your hair." I reached for a phone book, scanning the business pages. He slammed his fist down on the book.

"Shut up and listen, Lily."

I raised my eyebrows at his words. Wow. Mr. Calm and Blasé did have a temper. A ferocious battle brewed in the lines of his mouth and forehead. I recognized the signs. Nick used to look just like that when he was angry. And the one time he dared to touch me during a fury was the very last time he had ever laid his paws on my skin.

Bryce would never get that chance. I drew up to my full height, lacking as it was, and spit out, "Don't. Touch. Me."

His head reared back as though I slapped him. "What?"

Ice in my tone, I said, "You have a right to be angry, but if you lay one finger on me, I'll come at you with a circular saw and nail gun. Are we clear?"

He blinked. And frowned. And blinked again. "Jesus Christ, Lily. Someone hit you."

"Nick did, once, and he was lucky not to pull away a stub for a hand," I announced, as calmly as my constricting throat would allow.

A strange look came over him. Somewhere between rage and grief. "No, he's lucky he's already dead," Bryce muttered.

"Well, now you know. I won't suffer through that again. And it's best if you just let me go to a hotel until tomorrow."

"No."

I laughed bitterly. "I'm afraid you don't have a choice. You can't keep me here. That's kidnapping."

He smiled slightly. "I'm not kidnapping you. I only want you to listen for a second without interrupting."

I huffed and crossed my arms. "Fine. I'm listening, but if you're just going to yell at me, I'd prefer it if you kept it down. You have neighbors, you know."

"I'm not going to yell at you," he said hotly, belying his words. I arched an eyebrow. He inhaled deeply. "Lily, I am very upset with you, because I saw a woman today that looked nothing like the mud-splattered girl I met a few days ago. I am upset because you changed."

I put my fists on my hips. "Well, I couldn't exactly wear jeans and sneakers to that fancy restaurant, now could I?"

"I'm not talking about the damn dress!"

Another arch of my brow. "Get to the point, Mr. King. I have a cab to call."

"I'm talking about the filthy, playing in the dirt, able to fix a tree house, swinging from the rafters Lily Watson. The woman I'm falling in love with…"

Mother of God. "Wh-what?"

He stepped closer and smoothed his fingers along my cheek, gently, carefully. "You came through that door tonight looking like all the women I've ever known: dressed to kill and made up like some kind of airbrushed lingerie model. And though you were more beautiful, and sexier, than any of those other women, I hated it. I hated you for what you did to yourself."

My lungs wouldn't function to full capacity. His touch burned my skin. I felt hot and shivered. "I'm sorry. Wh-what did you just say?"

"You've never embarrassed me," he murmured instead of answering, cupping my face with both hands. "But I see you now as you should be. Your hair in that God-awful ponytail and your face clean of all makeup, and I want you. I've wanted women before, but never to the point where my body, my heart, hell, my brain ache. I want to make love to you until we are both too exhausted to even breathe. I want to taste every part of you, feel your heat and wetness, look down at you as our bodies slide together. I want—"

His next words never passed his lips. I took control of them, smothering him with all the pent-up passion of a woman possessed. The second I'd caught him staring at the cleavage escaping a wet towel, I suspected that he saw me as a real woman; different from the dirty tomboy he met a few days ago. But this? I would have never expected this.

He didn't really love me. He was confused. But at that moment, I didn't care. I ached, too.

I know I usually came across as confident and assertive, a woman that regularly experienced mind-boggling orgasms. But that was all a farce. Even with Nick, I looked at sex as a necessary part of being married. I enjoyed it – I did – but with all my big talk about great sex, it had been a really, *really* long time since the word "great" described my sexual encounters.

Still, if Bryce didn't make love to me that instant, he would discover a side of me *I* had never seen before.

169

"Lily," he whispered as I drew back. "Don't tease me. I can't stand it."

"Upstairs," I commanded. "Now."

He frowned, then grinned, swept me up another smothering kiss, and said, "Yes, Daisy."

~~~~~

She stripped as she ran up in front of him. Robe belt, robe, pink top, pink shorts... one glance at her panty-clad bottom – and nothing else – and he wasted no time following suit. He shed his clothes on the stairs as he kissed that pouty mouth, and they stumbled into the first bedroom they came across, tumbling onto the mattress, tangled and twisted and kissing together. Lily hooked her fingers around his hips and locked her legs behind him, her body molding and arching against him.

Her softly padded muscles flexed under her skin, warm and soft and fresh, and Bryce couldn't decide if he preferred the malleable roundness of her breasts or the firm ripples of her abs, since both areas attracted his touch, and he see-sawed his mind between loving the soft and being fascinated by the solid. "God, you feel wonderful," she moaned as her own hands taunted him with feathery touches and needy, massaging motions while she writhed under him. "Lily," he moaned back, nibbling on her neck, pulling her hair free from that ponytail and running his fingers through the damp strands, bringing them to his nose to inhale the sweet fragrance of her shampoo. His hands fled down her lean body, tugging the cotton barrier around her hips, wanting to go exploring and feel the warmth and smoothness of her skin all over. "Sweet Lily," he whispered again as she kicked off her panties and flipped on top of him.

Only the pale moonlight shone through the window, but he could see her clearly. The outline of her, hair spilling over her shoulders, the feminine curves of her breasts thrusting upward and the gentle dip of her waist flaring out in lovely hips - a flat, washboard stomach, and the sharp definition of muscular thighs and strong calves, not to mention the feminine muscle tone of her arms. This was a woman with stamina, and he couldn't wait to test her endurance.

"Lily..."

"Yes, Bryce," she said, leaning forward to rub the tips of her nipples over his chest, moaning with pleasure. He forgot what he wanted to tell her. His arousal throbbed and ached under her, feeling her slick folds massaging him as she sat atop him, but he couldn't bring himself to dive into her just yet. He needed to feel her, kiss her, worship the parts of her he could only glimpse in the dim light. She kissed his mouth, his neck, his ear, murmuring soft words of need.

"Lily..." he said again, just to hear the sound of her name again.

"Shhh," she said, placing a finger over his lips. "I've got you right where I've always wanted you. I haven't done this in a long time, but there are a few things I haven't forgotten."

Her lips moved over him at lightening speed, licking his chest and moving lower until her mouth found its target and his head emptied and burst with pleasure. He sucked in a breath, sitting upright as he threaded his fingers through her hair, and let it out with a whoosh. "I like your memory." She giggled and the reverberations did magical things to him. The pressure grew too intense. His blood boiled, and his pulse spiked, and his vision grew blurry, and his brain sparked with over-active synapses, but he held on. Just barely. Finally, she slithered up and grinned at him. His fingers curled into her hair and he pressed her lips to his, darting his tongue into the sweetness of her mouth.

Bryce rolled them over. "My turn," he whispered hoarsely and winked.

"Oh, I don't know." she groaned. "I'm ready. Take me."

He tested that theory, slipping a finger into the slick moisture that soaked her thighs, and he nearly obeyed her. But no. She had tormented him…it was her turn.

Her eyes rolled back into her head as his fingers caressed the depths of her. He took a breast in his mouth, nipping the hard button in its center until she squirmed with suffering. Then he moved to the other breast as he teased the little bud hidden in her curls.

"Bryce…please…"

"Not yet, sweetheart." He dipped his head, bestowing the pleasure she gave him – she tasted like the nectar of a honeysuckle blossom – and her moans gradually multiplied until they left her in a single rumble, and he felt her knees tighten around him, compressing his ribcage too tightly for comfort.

"Stop! Oh, God, Bryce!" she panted. "If you don't

stop, I'm going to...to...oh!...oh! *God!*" Every muscle in her body constricted and arched and stiffened as a keen wail drifted out from her throat. Spasms overtook her, and Bryce almost drowned in the flowing ambrosia that coated his tongue and lips. Her thighs sagged while he pushed her a little further, but he finally left her melting in a pool of sated flesh and bone to open the side table and rip off a condom from the stashed strip. She saw him through a dazed smile and in an instant, clarity resumed, and she moved away, hastily covering her breasts with her hands.

"Just how many women have you screwed in this bed?" she demanded angrily, a slight slur in her words.

He blinked at the sudden change and burst into laughter. "None, Lily. I like to keep my guests supplied."

She didn't believe him; he could tell. Her eyes flashed with that crystallized fire and her perfect, pouty mouth thinned to a mere line across her face.

"I promise you, Lily. The last time I made love to a woman, Kristen insisted that I was properly showered, shaved, and that the sheets were freshly laundered. She was not the type of woman to attack me in my guest house."

Lily listened, the fire not dimming a single flame. "Who's Kristen? And how long ago was this laundry day?"

Bryce sighed heavily. Every time he imagined Lily in her exact and present position, his brain never included this particular conversation. "You're upset," he said. "Maybe this wasn't such a good idea."

If anything, the blue flames intensified. "I am upset, but this – right here -- not being a good idea? That thought has yet to cross my mind. I just want to know who the hell Kristen is."

He sat back on his heels, resting against one of the posts at the end of the bed. He hoped she knew what she was asking for. "Kristen was my girlfriend, until she dumped me last week." And when it looked like she wanted more, he said, "She is a fashion designer and wears six-inch heels every day, and she is a towering five-eight with blonde hair, green eyes, and has a really terrible habit of picking the croutons out of her salads. Laundry day was exactly ten days ago, in her apartment, at exactly nine-fifteen at night. Any later and she would miss her favorite television show on the Style channel. I worked late that day, and Kristen was always willing, if not eager, to ease my frustrations. But I never loved her.

"The last person to stay in this room was a congressman out of Oregon who was seventy-six years old and retired every night at seven o'clock. In fact, the very last time a woman within twenty years of my age stepped into this room was most likely on Thursday, when Maria comes in to dust and air out the place."

He waited impatiently for any response. She was tortuously teasing him, sitting across from him, naked as the day she was born and more beautiful and surreal than anyone he had ever laid eyes on. No one had ever confused him more. Lily was pigheaded and went looking for fights, but underneath all that hardcore muscle and rough calluses was a soft woman who could turn his heart in flips with a simple smile and a quirked eyebrow.

"Why did she dump you?" she asked suddenly.

"Does it matter? I'm not seeing anyone right now."

Her lip twitched as though she wanted to smile. "I need to know if you have some whacked out habit that I don't know about."

Bryce realized the moment was over. He stood and began dressing.

"What are you doing?" Lily's voice came out clear, but a hint of desperation marbled the tone.

"I'm sorry, Lily," Bryce said after he tugged his shirt over his head. "I was about to make the sweetest love to you and explore your body in ways I could never grow tired of, but you want to ask questions."

Finally clothed, he resumed his spot on the bed, throwing a thick quilt over to her. "And I can't answer them if all I am thinking about is you naked, and me naked, and us together naked." He stopped to shake the image. "See, I'm distracted anyway, but at least I'm not naked. Go ahead, ask away."

Lily ignored the quilt. She sat up on her knees in front of him, her breasts bobbing with the movement. Bryce's mouth went dry. She wriggled closer and bent over, placing her hands on the bed in front of her.

"So I can ask anything, and you will tell me?"

"You can ask," he clarified.

"Why did she dump you?" Lily repeated.

"She saw me having lunch with another woman."

Lily's eyebrow arched, "Cheating?"

"No," he arched his own eyebrow, "business."

"And she dumped you for that? What kind of

business?"

His head fell against the post and he heaved another sigh. "No, she dumped me because that particular woman is a known cougar, and Kristen was jealous of what might happen. She only stuck around because of my money, and I only kept her because I hated having to search for dates when I need one. She dumped me because she didn't have the guts to fight for me. And I was happy to see her go. I don't want a woman that doesn't want me."

Lily chewed her lips. He focused on her face, not her body, although his body was miserable and missing hers badly and threatening to make that fact known. The fury in her eyes died and she smiled sheepishly at him. "Do I get another question?"

"Shoot."

"Why aren't you naked again?"

His head tilted down to look at her better. Her fingers were already going for his pants and shirt. "I thought you were mad," he began, and then, spying the devilish grin flash, he asked silkily, "So, does that mean I get a do-over?"

"No. No do-overs," she urged, pulling him to her. "You just have to start where you left off. Because if you don't get inside me now and do some of that exploring, I just might get angry."

That was all the encouragement he needed. The clothes came right back off, condom rolled on, and he plummeted into her. Lily froze.

"Did I hurt you?"

"God, no. You feel so good. Don't stop!"

"Make up your mind, Lily," he chuckled. "Stop...don't stop..." She shoved her pelvis securely onto him, locking her ankles around his waist. Her inner muscles tightened to the point of erotic pain and his head dropped to her breast. He groaned as he withdrew and slid slowly into her again, noting every ripple of her clenched muscles as he passed them.

"Oh hell, do that again," he cried.

"Do what?"

The ripple effect of her female muscles undulated against him. "That," he said, thrusting roughly inside her. "Again."

Lily waved around him, and he buried himself to the hilt to feel every swell and furrow of her muscles rolling up and down his length.

"God," he whispered seductively in her ear, "I could come just from that."

"Not yet, you don't," she giggled, stopping her tantalizing motions. "Not so fast."

Lily rocked under him slowly, but soon the feel of her enveloping center captured his composure, and they found a rhythm that threatened to give them both heart attacks, yet neither seemed to notice. "I love you," he whispered against her mouth. Without much more effort, the quickening of their orgasms met and Bryce collapsed on Lily, catching his breath while she gasped against his chest.

Their hearts slowed, their lungs began to rise and fall normally, and Bryce moved his crushing weight off her body with the energy of a sloth. His eyelids drooped and he dreamily thought of sleep. Lily shifted against him, finding the latex sheathe, stripped him of it and tossed it in a wastebasket.

"Thank you," he mumbled.

"Thank me later," she whispered and fastened her fingers around his sated member. He opened his eyes to look curiously at her in the dark. Her hair was a tangled mess around her head, and her cheeks were flushed with satisfaction. *Beautiful...surreal.*

"Lily?"

She tipped the corner of her mouth up, lowering her face close to his. Her hot breath tickled his cheek. "Again."

~~~~~

Bryce rolled over in his sleep -- what little he got -- feeling the bed next to him. Cold sheets met his hand. His eyes blinked open. Lily was gone.

Chapter Fourteen

"**Y**ou're home," Ann squealed when I answered the door chime that afternoon.

"Yeah, for only about ten minutes," I complained. "How do you do that?"

"Do what? Know where you are at all times? Whom you're with? What you're doing?" She shrugged and bounded into my house. "I'm psychic."

If that were true, she would have called me last night sometime in the midst of Bryce making love to me. I had no idea where that man got his energy in bed. I could run circles around him during the day, but at night, he literally wore me out. That last time, he made love to me with such deliberate perfection, my orgasms came and went without either of us noticing. Not until he plunged one final thrust, did I realize that my limbs shook.

He whispered that he loved me all over again, and my heart clenched. Leaving him was possibly the cruelest thing I had ever done, but our worlds would never meet. Bryce King didn't love me. Not Lily Watson, the tomboy from a modest background. He was a charismatic millionaire with money and women falling like a snowstorm all around him, and I was a sarcastic ditch-digger who had been burned by love one time too many. He was much better off without me.

Did I love him?

I didn't have an answer for that. I liked him. I liked him a lot. But love? I just couldn't be sure. We did not know each other well enough, and, categorically, breathtaking sex could never substitute for the real thing.

"So? How was Dallas?" Ann asked with such pointed sweetness that I knew she suspected something.

"Hot."

"And Mr. King? How was he?"

"Polite."

"No, Lily, really. *How* was he?"

I shrugged past her into the laundry room where I was dumping my dirty clothes into the washer. "Ann, is there a point to this visit?"

"Yes," she jumped up to sit on the dryer. "I want to know about the sex."

"What sex?"

"The sex you and our Mr. King had together," she grinned at me.

"So, he's *our* Mr. King? You are married; you realize that, don't you?"

"I'm quite aware of it, as Bently reminded me last night—"

"Stop!" I held up a hand in her face. "I don't want to know what you do with your husband. I do have to work with the guy."

"Over and over and over again," she finished, still grinning wickedly. I groaned and turned the dial on the washer. "Speaking of Bently, he told me to remind you about movie night tonight. He said that just because you've been out of town for a few days, you're still not off the hook."

"My ex-husband is dead," I growled. "And if I was married to yours, he'd be dead, too."

Ann sighed. "Yeah, he's pretty callous sometimes,

but he's kind of determined to have movie night tonight." She examined her nails with such obvious earnestness, frowning over the cuticles.

"Okay, I give. What does he have planned?"

She popped to the ground, her red curls bouncing with her. "He's bringing a friend." I jerked to a stop, forgetting what Bently told me on Saturday, and she ran up in back of me.

"Oh, no."

"No one you know. His name is Tommy, something or another. They're in the same bowling league together or something. Bently said he moved to town a few weeks ago. He said that he's divorced, two children that live with their mother, and he's a fireman. Just think, Lily! A fireman! The fantasies! I know I've had a few. And he's blonde, just the way you like them."

"Again, stop."

"Well, it's not like you hit it off with Mr. Rich and Polite. This could be good for you. Go on a date…get to know each other…get laid…" She perched her bottom on my kitchen counter.

"I don't need to get laid. I'm good," I grumbled, scanning the open refrigerator for something to eat. A visit to the grocery store was long overdue.

"Ah ha!" Ann exclaimed, pointing a finger at me. "You did have sex with him!"

"Really, Ann, I don't want to talk about it."

"Come on," she whined behind me. "Tell me something. Did you jump him that first night, or did you wait? I bet he's a boxers man."

"Jockies," I supplied, smiling to myself. Ann

squealed again, clapping like a little girl.

"Tell me more!"

"Not a chance."

She slid off the counter and wrapped her arms around me. "Please, Lil Lil? Please, please, pretty please? With sugar and cinnamon and chocolate fudge on top?"

"I'm not giving you every sordid detail," I told her.

"Okay, then just the clean ones," she tried. I pinched my lips together in mock silence and threw the key over my shoulder.

"Alright," she squared her shoulders, "then I'll ask him." She reached for the phone. I knocked it out of her hand.

"Fine. One detail."

"Yea!" she clapped again.

I crinkled my brow. She would get it out of me sooner or later. I should give her something to chew on. "But you can't tell anyone. And I mean *no one*."

"Not a word," she grinned.

"He told me he loved me."

Ann's face fell to the floor. Her typical cheerfulness evaporated with the quickness of a sprinting cheetah. "That bastard," she growled.

My eyes widened. "Ann!"

"Well, he is! He told you he loved you just to get you in the sack! I've known men like him my whole life. He's a rat bastard that deserves to be hung with fishing line over a pit of starving, vampire, mutant piranhas."

I suppressed a giggle and bit into an apple. "I think you're exaggerating a little bit."

"Okay, then tell me this. Did he say the dirty little

words before or after you had sex?" She snatched my apple, biting into the opposite side.

"Hey! That's my last one!"

"Answer the question, Lil Lil."

I seized my apple from her grasp and smiled ruefully. "Both, actually. Before and after. And during, for your information."

Her little pug nose crinkled as she pursed her lips. "Fine, then maybe he does."

"Nope," I wagged my head in denial. "He doesn't love me. He's mistaken. Confused and probably regretting the words even as we speak. Perhaps he did say them because he wanted to sleep with me, but he didn't have to. I'd been clenching my thighs together since day one."

Ann pressed her tongue to her cheek. "That good, huh?"

I gave her a sharp look. "I did say I wasn't going to discuss this with you, right?"

"Yeah, but you always do," she grinned.

~~~~~

Not in a good mood at all, Bryce pushed his way through reporters to his office, with *The Dallas News* tucked under his arm. Jacobson, his PR man, had some serious explaining to do.

Gloria met him at her desk. "I take it you saw the paper?"

"How could I miss a headline like this?" He slapped the crumpled paper down on the nearest surface. Bold print shouted, "Murder Secures Business Deal."

"Get Jacobson in here now."

"He's already on his way," she replied.

Bryce nodded and stomped into his office. Justin looked up from a file he was poring over and grimaced. "I'd say, 'Good morning,' but I won't."

"How did this happen?"

"A freak coincidence," Justin said. "A reporter was at the police station, getting comments for a different story, and overheard some detective discussing the Garcia case with colleagues. It took off from there."

Bryce dropped into his desk chair and picked up a pen. A second later, it flew across the room and smashed into the wall. "Son of a...! Christ!" He stabbed a hand through his hair and thought, hurriedly doing damage control in his head.

"Okay," Bryce resigned. "The police are obviously incompetent enough to gossip while reporters are around. We need to figure this one out on our own. Do we still have that private investigator on retainer?"

"Martin Prescott? Yeah, I called him early this morning," Justin said. "He'll be here at ten."

"Good," Bryce said, and Jacobson entered. And stopped. And swallowed. His employer scowled at him.

"Bryce," George Jacobson said, "I've already sent out a statement, and my department is looking into the leak."

"A statement?" Bryce asked coolly. "I'm giving you one day to get this mess cleared up. One day. Or you won't have a department to go back to. Do I make myself clear?"

Jacobson gulped loud enough for it to echo across the building and down the elevator. "Yes, Mr. King."

He left, and Justin eyed Bryce evenly. "Was that necessary? George has been with us since the beginning. He's good at his job. This wasn't his fault."

Again, Bryce wondered why he ever insisted on becoming friends with his employees. He always felt guilty reprimanding them. "You're right," he sighed, and buzzed Gloria. "Call Jacobson back. I need to apologize to him."

To Justin, he said, "Can you take care of Prescott? Whatever he needs, get it to him. Find out who killed Garcia, and try to keep it quiet. I don't want wind of this to get back to Lily. She's suffered enough."

Justin frowned at him, pacing vigorously. "Lily Watson?"

"Is there another Lily that was previously married to Garcia?"

Justin raised his palms up at Bryce's curt tone. "No need to get pissed. I'm just curious about why her feelings should matter to you."

Bryce didn't answer. How could he? The woman he fell crazily in love with up and disappeared on him. He closed his eyes and saw her exquisite blue eyes gazing up at him with passion and devotion. Sweat soaked his palms and he clenched his fists. Lily had snuck out that morning, a clear indication of how little he meant to her, and his irritation had nothing to do with newspapers or department leaks. He opened himself up, said the scary words, and received only barren pain for his gamble.

She didn't love him. That was fine. Just dandy. It was better this way. He didn't want a woman that didn't want him.

"Hey, man," Justin interrupted his thoughts. "What's going on with you two?"

Bryce breathed in one solid breath. "Nothing. Absolutely nothing."

~~~~~

Two weeks later...

"Mr. King?" Gloria asked again. Bryce glanced up from his computer to look at her. His secretary started her usual morning report with her customary efficiency, but some time after the first few updates, he'd stopped listening. Lily's face smiled back at him from his computer screen. Watson Construction had a small website – barely more than a single page – and her picture, along with her father's, graced the homepage.

The photo had been taken a couple of years ago, and Lily looked younger, smoother, fresher...and seemingly happier than the Lily he knew. The picture on the screen was so similar to how she looked when he had made love to her, and his body reacted accordingly. Had it really been almost two weeks since he last saw her? Last touched her?

"Mr. King," Gloria said to regain his attention.

"Go ahead, Gloria. I'm listening."

"No, you are not. I just told you that your stocks took a two point hit and you never batted an eye."

Bryce looked at her again. "I'm sorry. What were we

talking about?"

Gloria sighed and closed her folder. She took off her glasses and stared at him square in the eye. "Go home, Mr. King. You should take some time off. Maria says that you haven't been sleeping or eating."

"Maria says? I should remind you that neither of you is my mother."

"Well, someone has to look after you. Your mother would roll over in her grave if she knew you were treating yourself this way. You're a mess. Ever since you went to Arkansas, you have been distracted. Jacobson cleared the company's name and sued the *News* for slander, but it's not like you to ignore your work this way." She went on and on, lecturing him, but his eyes traveled back to Lily and he shut her out again.

No contact from her in two weeks. Not a single word. After suffering through that first day without her, he went home, wandered through his empty rooms, fell across the bed she slept in those two nights and nearly wept. He hung up his pride and tried to call her, just to hear her voice again, but her answering machine picked up the first three times. After that, he received the "no longer in service" message, and she had changed her cell phone number as well. He left messages at her work number, but she never called him back.

The only way he could see her, short of flying back to Little Rock, was through his computer monitor. He searched all the online communities like a crazed stalker, and still he came up short. For someone with a computer science degree, her presence was absent from the Internet.

Lily, where are you? What are you doing?

Remembering what he had told Justin, "nothing" was a lie. Everything was going on between him and Lily. She just didn't know it yet.

"...didn't have the guts to fight for me..." Those words haunted him. After two days of appearing indifferent to the rest of the world and almost believing it himself, he just couldn't do that any more. He realized he'd become just like Kristen; become his own worst nightmare. He'd become a man that didn't have the backbone to fight for love.

He would do anything – absolutely anything! – to hold Lily in his arms right that moment. He wanted to fight, but she wasn't letting him. He wanted to go caveman and haul her back to him, but Lily, being Lily, was making it difficult.

Bryce didn't know what to do. He'd never had to fight for a woman. Like Lily told him, women fell into his lap. Money-grabbing "ladies" attached themselves to him like opposing sides of a Velcro strip. The usual ideas seemed too predictable. Flowers. Candy. Love letters. Shopping sprees. Lily Watson was anything but predictable. He could almost picture her shoving a dozen roses down her garbage disposal with a giant wooden spoon, all the while spewing obscenities in hope that Bryce's ears burned to a crisp.

He smiled at that and, from the corner of his eye, spied Gloria leaving his office in a huff. Good. He needed some peace to ponder Lily.

Justin flew into his office a while later. "You skipped the meeting," he announced.

"Meeting?"

"Yes, the shareholder meeting. It was this afternoon. They were not pleased."

"I'm sure you handled them," Bryce muttered.

His friend cocked his head and said matter-of-factly, "It's seven o'clock."

Bryce looked at his watch. He had lost the entire day hunting for Lily. He scrubbed a hand through his hair. "I don't know what's happening to me. All I can think about is her."

Justin nodded and sat in one of the couches by the eastern window. "I can understand that. She's some woman."

Bryce's face hardened, and Justin smirked. "Listen, Bryce," he said calmly, "she's not like any other woman you've ever known. Or any I've known. If you weren't so obvious from the start, *and* I wasn't married, I would have charmed her. Made her mine. But let's face it. She's a Daisy, and you don't want to get involved with a woman like that."

"*She is not a Daisy!*" Bryce growled, thinking about how he called her Daisy right before he made love to her.

"Just as I thought," Justin claimed. "But Daisy doesn't want you. Otherwise, you would have heard from her by now. Face it, man. She's gone. You've got a company to run, eager women willing to take Lily's place, golf balls to hit. Get on with your life. Lily did."

Bryce glared at him through a fiery glaze of fury. Justin had been his friend for years, and he had never once been angry with him. But now, Bryce imagined himself choking the life out of his friend.

The realization hit him in the chest, and he inhaled a cooling breath. "You don't understand…"

"Oh, I understand all right. You're in love with her. I know the look. I've seen it on my own face whenever I think about Emily."

Bryce turned his head in disgust. "Is there something else you wanted to tell me besides commenting on my foolish behavior?"

"Yeah, Prescott returned from Oklahoma this afternoon. Remember? We sent him there because of all those flights Garcia made in the last three months?"

Bryce barely remembered what he had for lunch. "Go on," he urged.

"He came back with a lead. But you're not going to like it. It seems that someone else was flying out to Oklahoma City at the same time."

"Just get on with the soap opera," Bryce grunted. Please don't say Lily. Please don't say…

"Vivian."

Bryce stared at him. "Vivian? Vivian Corter?"

"Now, Vivian Morrissey," Justin explained. "She got married to Benjamin Morrissey a few weeks ago. They eloped in Vegas."

"No, that's not right," Bryce exclaimed. "I saw her prenup. She was marrying Colonel Stephens."

Justin shook his head. "Nope. She lied. She eloped with Morrissey."

Shards of ice pricked his skin. Benjamin Morrissey. The man that wanted Bryce's blood. The husband of the woman that killed herself only days after Bryce sternly refused to sleep with her. The man that owned over twenty percent of King Enterprises' shares, the third largest chunk of ownership next to Justin's and Bryce's.

The man now married to Vivian, combining shares to create the thirty percent needed for partnership, according to the company's shareholding bylaws.

"That's not good," Bryce commented dimly.

"You don't say? You should have been at that meeting. Morrissey submitted all the paperwork. You and I have exactly sixty days to file against him, but to do that, we'll need something on him." Justin sighed heavily and stopped moving for the first time in the last ten minutes. "I don't know about you, but I don't have a single grain of dirt on the man."

"Keep looking," Bryce said and turned back to Lily's picture. Problems within his company were mounting but all he could seem to care about was what Lily was doing at that moment. Probably scaling a second-story roof, just trying to break her fool neck.

Justin eyed his friend for a few minutes. "Did I ever tell you about the time I met Emily? It was in a bar, of all things. I was with another woman. Eve, I think her name was. But one look at Emily, bending over a pool table, flirting with a bunch of cowboys, and I was hooked. I left Eve high and dry that night, a bastardly thing to do, but I never looked back."

"Do you have a point?" Bryce asked without looking up.

"We all become jackasses when it comes to our women. Emily has – and always will be – the love of my life. Lily is yours." He paused to let that sink in. Bryce looked at Lily's photo and his chest felt tight with need and sorrow.

Justin stood and straightened his suit jacket. "You are Bryce King, a man that has never let anything stand in the way of what he wants. If you want Lily Watson, then go get her. And for God's sake, do it quickly. I'm not going to hold up your end of this business forever." With that, he left his pained friend to contemplate his next move.

Chapter Fifteen

"It's supposed to rain tonight, really bad. Like tornado bad," Bently had stated earlier that Friday afternoon, as though no one could see the dark storm clouds moving in from the western horizon. I reclined under our little shade tree, picking at my lunch, and threw a scornful glare at him.

Bently was not on my good side today, or any of the past week's worth of days. He continuously pushed that Thomas guy at me, thinking we would hit it off eventually. *Fat chance.*

Fireman Thomas, I snorted, was a blonde, conceited, ill-mannered man in the shell of an underwear model's body. And he knew it. If he'd ever worked a hard day in his life, I would eat my hammer. Whatever tales Thomas had been telling people, he was no firefighter. Smooth palms and buffed nails were not the result of rescuing small children from burning flames or wielding one of those giant water hoses.

When Bently brought him to our Movie Night, he took one look at me and licked his lips! Like I was some kind of ice cream cone, dripping with a desire to be sucked on. After I finally pushed both of them out of my house, my palms itching so terribly all night from the yearning to slap someone, I turned on Ann and gave her the bitching of the year.

And Ann grinned all through it. Then, I wanted to slap her, but I refrained. She was my best friend and didn't deserve the backlash of her husband's uninvited intentions. Subsequently, I failed to answer his next riddle the following Friday, and had to endure Fireman

Thomas all over again. Today would be different. If I answered correctly – and on time – I would get to command the next Movie Night. But if I didn't, I'd sell my house and move to Bali before next Wednesday.

"Just tell me your damn riddle," I snapped.

"Such words, Lily!"

"Bently…I'm warning you now…"

He held up a palm, grinning stupidly, and said, "Okay, okay. What is as big as you are, but doesn't weigh anything?"

"Your shadow," I answered without delay. Bently's grin slipped.

"You cheated. You asked Ann what I was going to say, didn't you?"

"Nope," I said, standing and brushing the dirt from my jeans. "You asked that one back in May."

"Oh…so I did," he frowned. That expression looked odd on him. "Alright. Then I get a new one—"

"Nope again. *That's* cheating. If you can't keep up with your own riddles, that's not my fault. And don't even think of inviting Thomas."

"Aw, come on, Lily. He likes you. Give the guy a chance."

"Not even on a cold day in hell. The guy's a toad." I cast a cheeky sneer at him. "We're watching *'Fried Green Tomatoes'*."

"No!" he shot to his feet. "Please, anything but that! We can watch *The Princess Bride* again. Or *Dirty Dancing*," he begged urgently, "Or *Titanic*. That's a good one—"

"Sorry, Bently. 'Secret's in the sauce,'" I patted his cheek and walked away, his keening moan increasing as he continued to suggest other "chick flicks." I grinned. Possibly, this day would have its good moments.

Back at the shack, I slumped in my tiny chair behind my miniscule work desk, feeling the pressure of the upcoming storm bear down on me. And, oddly, the winds kicking up outside weren't what bothered me. Fifteen days had passed since I laid eyes on Bryce. When I woke up that morning to see his hand covering my breast and a self-appreciative smile on his sleeping face that screamed, "I'm the man!," I ran.

Luckily, all my clothes were still packed from when Maria moved them into the guesthouse. I threw on some jeans and a shirt and rushed from his home as fast as I could, not bothering to call a cab until I was well away. By the time I finished witnessing Nick's burial and waited in line to be admitted through the airport's security gate, Bryce had called my cell phone five times.

I listened to the first message, *Lily, why didn't you wake me? We could have done this together. Please, call me,* and the second, *There is something wrong, isn't there? Was it something I did? Lily, call me back so we can talk about this. I need to hear your voice. Call me, please.* I turned my phone off after that, but then changed my mind and switched it to vibration, just in case Daddy or Momma needed to talk to me. But I deleted every future voice mail from Bryce without hearing them.

And I'll be the first to admit it. Bryce scared the living crap-ola out of me. I was falling for him, and I didn't need that right now. Christ! I'd just watched my ex-husband get turned into worm food! How could I even consider being with another man? The indecency of it refreshed my guilt. Daddy had always said there was something wrong with me. I was dropped on my head as a baby? Or I inhaled too many paint fumes?

To feel lust, guilt, shame, anger, and more lust for the same man wasn't healthy. Right? And why, of all people, did it have to be *him*? There were a lot of nice men in my own area. Lots of single, hard-working, blue-collar men looking for a woman to cuddle up to at night.

But no, I had to go and get involved with a tie-wearing, power-tool-incompetent, don't-know-his-Philips-from-his-flathead millionaire. On the short flight back to Little Rock, I think I may have worried a few of the other passengers with my heated grumblings and ferocious glares. That man in the checked shirt was surely an air marshal. He kept his eyes glued to the back of my head.

Then that night, I endured Thomas the firefighter for the first time, juggling my patience between him and the ever-constant beeping of my answering machine. Ann answered the first phone call and motioned me over. Somehow, I knew who it was, hung up, and disconnected the phone from the wall jack. All the phones. Ann eyed me oddly, but did not comment.

I was determined to erase Bryce King from my mind. I had never fallen for that type of man, and I didn't want to be that woman; the type that sits around on the veranda, sipping mimosas and reading *Vanity Fair*, all the while waiting for Bryce to come home to me.

No, I needed to get my hands dirty. And I dreamed

of finding someone who wouldn't be afraid to do the same. I thought that person was Nick, but it turned out that he was all show. Then I stopped looking.

The problem with Bryce was that his idea of getting his hands dirty included shaking hands with a Democrat. *I* was Democrat, well, more so than anything else. But politics aside, he would always be the man in the immaculately pressed suit and I would always be the girl in ratty blue jeans, crawling through the mud. With such obvious differences in our preferred lifestyles, how could we possibly be together?

I sighed back in my desk chair and attempted to push aside his memory. As the old country saying goes, "Want in one hand, spit in the other. See which fills up faster," I was determined to stop spitting...period.

Outside the shack, the wind whistled through the miniscule gaps around the windows. Bently was right; a bad storm was coming. I considered letting everyone go early – just in case – when I heard a knock on the shabby door.

"Come in!"

Daddy had closed himself in his office that morning, and I hadn't heard a word from him since. He had spent most days quietly brooding since I came home. Michael took a sick day, so the office duties were left up to me. I expected Eddie or Miguel to ask me about leaving early, as they routinely do on Fridays. Instead, two policemen entered.

"Can I help you?"

"Is Henry Watson here?"

"Um, yes. Can I ask what this is about?" I stood

slowly, dread soaking into my blood. Daddy came out of his office then, and the policemen turned to him.

"Henry James Watson?"

"Yes," he answered. The shorter policeman removed handcuffs from his belt loop.

"Henry Watson, you are under arrest for the murder of Nicholas Garcia. You have the right to remain silent. Anything you say can and will be used against you..." The officer continued with the Miranda rights while shackling my father's wrists behind his back.

"Daddy?"

He turned his sad eyes to me. "It's okay, Lil Lil. Call your mother."

They escorted him out of the shack to a police cruiser. All construction stopped as workers shambled closer to watch. "Bently," I shouted. He ran to me. "Hand out paychecks. They're in Daddy's top drawer. Then send everyone home and lock up for the night."

"Where are you going?"

"To straighten out this mess," I called, racing to my truck as the first splats of heavy rain sprinkled the ground.

~~~~~

"Gloria!" Bryce shouted as soon as Justin disappeared. "Are you still here?"

"Of course, I am," she spoke, coming into his office. Did that woman have any kind of life outside of this place?

"Get me the first flight to Little Rock," Bryce

commanded, stuffing papers into his briefcase.

"I'm sorry, Mr. King. There is a storm heading that way. All flights in the area have been grounded until further notice."

"And you know this how?"

She raised her chin and smiled secretly. "I tried to book a flight an hour ago."

He considered that. Then he surprised her with a hug. "How long does it take to drive there?"

"About six hours, I think," she answered, smothered in his embrace. "But the weather channel says it's a bad storm. There's a possibility of tornadoes. It'll take you all night."

He let her go. "That's more of a reason to get there quickly. Lily will most likely stand out in her front yard, daring anything to touch her house."

Gloria straightened her glasses. "I really need to meet this woman. She sounds fascinating."

"You have no idea." Bryce kissed her cheek and rushed to the elevators.

His Porsche made good time until he had left Texarkana behind him. Then he hit the storm, and it seemed like earth and sky had changed places. Somewhere outside a little hole in the ground called Hope, he was forced to stop under an overpass as fist-sized hail plummeted from the sky, denting his car.

But he didn't care. Getting to Lily was all that mattered. He checked the GPS and learned that he still had about two hours of drive time, plus weather delays, before holding her again. He could see her now, outside in the driving rain, boarding up the windows of her house instead of hiding in her bathtub. Lily was most likely shooting daring glares over her shoulder at the storm, and just the image in his mind angered him.

"Lily, you idiot! Get inside!" He shouted northwards, as though she could somehow hear him. If she put herself in danger, he was going to give her one good talking to, that was for sure. A good yell that would make her eyes flash and a good kiss to smother her own arguments. His temper broiled at the thought of her trying to tough it out.

"Dammit, Lily!"

Another curse from his mouth. That woman drove him to use words he rarely said. After a few calming breaths, he soothed his mind with the reasoning that if anyone could survive a tornado threat, it would be Lily. She was as hard as nails, and any storm would be sorry to cross her. Still, as the hail lightened up enough to see the road, he slammed his foot on the clutch and shifted into gear, pushing his car to speed at record time. A few miles down the road, his cell phone rang.

"Where are you?" Justin's voice carried over the speakerphone, drowning out the storm.

"About two hours away." He glanced at the clock on the dashboard. It was after midnight.

"Well, you might as well find a place to crash for the night. Storm damage has shut down the interstate outside of Little Rock. And you will get yourself lost trying to detour down country roads. The next thing we know, we'll find your body hacked up behind some woodpile with a shirtless hillbilly playing a banjo on top."

Bryce smiled at that. His face felt tight. He had been clenching his jaw with impatience all night. Smiling hurt, but it was a relief. "I have GPS," he told his friend.

"Those things are unreliable," Justin argued. "Besides, I found out that Lily might not be home."

Bryce stared at the phone, taking his eyes off the road too long, and almost didn't notice the semi-truck he zoomed up behind. "How do you know that? Did you talk to her? How did you get her numbers? She changed them."

"I called her parents' house," Justin said. Why didn't he think of that? Oh, yeah, because calling her momma and begging for her to put in a good word for him was pathetic.

"And?"

"And well, " Justin cleared his throat, "You're not going to like this."

"What?" Panic fused his joints together and froze his muscles. Why was it that every time Justin said those words, a catastrophe was about to happen?

"Henry Watson was arrested this afternoon for Garcia's murder."

Bryce's foot eased off the accelerator. The Porsche slowed to a crawl, and he turned it onto the shoulder. At this rate, he would never get there.

"Did you talk to Lily?" he asked again.

"Yeah, I did. Her mother gave me her new cell number. She's not too happy about you heading in her direction."

"What did she say?"

"She mumbled something about dots only making a

bigger mess and how quickly she can get her hands on vampire piranhas. It was all very confusing. Do you want her number?"

"Yes."

Justin clicked off, and Bryce dialed Lily's number. "Hello?" her frantic voice called out to him and pierced his heart. The sounds of a vacuum cleaner and distant sirens mingled together in the background.

"Lily? Are you alright?" He had to shout over the noise.

"Bryce?! Are you crazy? I can't talk to you now!"

"Lily, please," he begged, "are you okay?"

"No, Bryce! I'm not okay! Daddy was arrested today *for murder,* and I have a tornado flying over top of my house! I'M NOT OKAY!"

A sharp crack and the sound of glass shattering had him seizing his phone, just wanting to be closer to her. "Lily!"

She shrieked and cursed. "Bryce?"

"I'm here, Lily," he panted, squeezing his eyes shut.

"I am glad you called, although I don't know how you got my number," Another clamor of cracks, pops, and rain pelting on windows broke through. "But there is one thing I've been wanting to tell you…"

A loud groan cut off any more words. Bryce yelled again, "Lily! Are you there?"

A few scattered heartbeats later, she answered, "Yes, I'm here. I just want to tell you…I…I quit!"

The phone went dead. Bryce didn't hesitate to think about what that meant. He put his car in gear and flew towards the capital city. Again and again he tried Lily's number, but she never answered. Fallen trees, clumps of debris and tractor-trailers set up as barricades littered the interstate as he got closer. Bryce maneuvered around each obstacle as though he had been driving through apocalyptic ruin his whole life.

Inside the metro area of Little Rock, there was a different story to tell. He had to input alternate routes to Lily's neighborhood on his GPS several times. Finally, he spotted familiar streets and storefronts. He was only a few blocks away. The storm had passed, but the carnage left in its wake had him fearing for Lily.

Flashing lights and a temporary roadblock stopped his progress down the street to her house. The damage in this part of town was extensive, and news crews were already on the scene. Shells of houses glared through the deathly black night; some were now lodging uprooted trees in their attics.

"Sorry, sir. You have to turn around," a policeman said to him through the open window.

"A friend of mine lives down here. She's not answering her phone," he said.

"We have crews checking all the houses," the uniform told him. "Which house is your friend in?"

"The brown and white one in the middle. Lily Watson," Bryce said.

The man called in the information over his radio, and then turned back to Bryce, "If she's home, we'll get to her. Call this number in the morning for her status." He held a card through the window. Bryce took it, and gazed down the street toward Lily's house, hoping to see her running to him, but he never did. The policeman urged him to leave.

Bryce couldn't seem to concentrate on anything besides Lily's unconscious body lying in a pile of rubble. He grappled with his fear, but eventually he couldn't stand not knowing.

"Hey! Get back here!"

Bryce ran down the street, ignoring the authoritative shouts. A spotlight bobbled behind him, lighting his way. He glanced over his shoulder, seeing one of the news crews following him. "Don't loose him," the reporter shouted to her cameraman. And for once, he was thankful for the publicity, if it meant granting him enough light to skirt around fallen tree limbs and broken-off parts of people's homes.

He neared Lily's home. His lungs hurt from the sprint down the street and from his dread. As the spotlight caught up with him, he received his first good look at the home she had so lovingly restored. Now it embraced a giant oak tree, one whole side smashed to a pile of brick and splintered wood, her old pick-up truck crushed into a heap of scrap metal.

"Oh, my God," he whispered to himself.

"Sir!" the pushy reporter shoved a microphone in his face. "Do you know who lives here? Was it family? A friend?" The woman scanned Bryce's face while he stared at Lily's house and tried to decide the easiest way to get inside.

"Wait a minute," she said. "Aren't you Bryce King?"

Bryce darted a look at her. She smiled with aggressive determination. "Do you know who killed Nicholas Garcia? What connection does your company have with his death? Is this the house of Lily Watson? Is Ms. Watson involved in the death of Mr. Garcia? Have you any comment concerning the arrest of Henry Watson? Is it true that you bought his company last month?"

After every question, she pushed the damp mic under his nose, but waited only long enough to think of another question before belting that at him. Bryce said nothing. He studied the wreckage again.

Where was she when he had called her? Her bedroom? Bathroom? Where would Lily go to be safe?

"Mr. King? Any comment at all?"

Bryce jerked the microphone from her hand and threw it over her shoulder into the street. "Now really," she muttered. He stepped around her, edging up the front yard. He could climb the tree trunk and drop in from the second floor. But only if the stairs were clear enough for him to go down them. Or he could try to crawl through one of the windows. Lily would kill him if he broke another one, but if that meant saving her...

He picked up a rock and poised to throw.

"You do that, and you're dead meat."

The rock fell from his fingers at the beautiful voice. She came from the side of her house with a fist on her hip and a huge monkey wrench pointed at him.

"Do you have any idea how hard it is to find one-hundred-year-old window glass?" Lily planted her feet in front of him. She was soaked to the bone, her ponytail strung down her back and dotted with glass shards. A purple knot stood out on her left temple. "What are you doing here?"

Relieved at seeing her approach safely and hearing her sardonic attitude, Bryce grinned foolishly down at her. "I came to save you."

Lily snorted and eyed the television people behind him. "Are they part of the rescue squad, too?"

"Nope, just me, but I can call some firemen or police over here."

She made another derisive sound deep in her throat. "I've had about all I can take of firemen. And the police for that matter. However," she pursed her lips, "you can get rid of *them*. They're stepping all over my hostas." She waved the reporter away and showed them her back.

"Lily, are you okay? Are you hurt?"

"It took me three years to restore that house," she sighed and fell to her knees on the wet grass. Her shoulders began to shake. Bryce sat down beside her and drew her body into his warmth, letting her cry.

Chapter Sixteen

I could only go up from here, right? There was no more distance to fall. In the span of two weeks, my life sped along a rollercoaster track, until finally plummeting into an abyss of grief, anger, and pain.

Daddy sat in a jail cell for murder. A tornado ripped my house in two. Bryce King lovingly wrapped his arms around my body while I cried into his shoulder.

I didn't know which was worse.

"Throw me a line here," I mumbled to myself.

Bryce shifted his head down to my cheek, "I beg your pardon?"

That was all it took. Four little words from his mouth, *those* words. Why did he have to always say that? What was wrong with, "Excuse me?" Or "What'd you say?" Or even "Speak up; I can't here you."

No, he had to say things that continuously clarified the difference between the two of us. I jumped to my feet, rounding on him. "What the hell are you doing here?"

He eyed me oddly. "I was worried about you."

"Worried about me? Why? I can take care of myself."

He stood slowly, drawing his brows together and clenching his jaw. "Lily, I just came five hundred miles to see you. Haven't you anything else to say than that?"

"Yes!" I spat at him. "You did this! If it weren't for you, none of this would have happened. Why can't you just leave me alone?"

He stepped so close that our bodies were almost touching. "You think I caused a tornado to wreck your home? I may have a lot of connections, but that is a little far fetched, even for me."

I pushed at his chest. He didn't budge. "Not my house, you jerk! I'm talking about my father. If you hadn't bought his company, he would be at home right now. Nick wouldn't be dead, and I wouldn't be standing in my yard in the middle of the night screaming at you! Go away! I don't want you here."

"Oh, this is good," muttered the news reporter, who still stood nearby with her camera aimed at us. "You are getting this, right?" she asked the man behind the camera. He nodded at her and frowned apologetically at me.

"And you, too!" I yelled at them. "Get off my property!" I pivoted back to my house, wanting to hide inside it. Seeing the beautiful pin oak crushing the whole right side down to the foundation, I threw my arms up in the air and slumped into myself. I didn't even have my cell phone handy; it was lying under the wreckage of my hallway. I couldn't call anyone to come get me.

"Come on, Lily," Bryce took my arm gently. "I'll drive you to whereever you need to go. Then you will never see me again if that is what you wish."

I jerked out of his grasp. But I had no other option. "Fine."

He led me down the street to his car. Mr. Scheemer's two-story Craftsman, boasting stunning architecture that drew eyes toward the wide porch and hefty stain-glassed entry, was untouched – thank God! But the Bartlett's muddy-brown Italian Renaissance looked worse than mine in the dim light. And the narrow cottage on the corner would need more than a miracle to restore it to full glory.

Bryce waited patiently and, as I gazed sorrowfully at all the lost beauty of my neighborhood, never once hurried me along. The dark night hid most of the ruin, but I knew. In a year, maybe, I could look at my neighbors' homes and not see the death around me. And at that moment, Bryce King took a back seat to the worst on my list. Still, I knew that what I was experiencing here would not be in the same emotional arena as when I would walk through Daddy's front door and realize he wasn't there.

Bryce kept quiet as he drove out of the city to the little community across the river where Momma and Daddy lived for thirty years. Once, their house had been my home. Now, it seemed, it was the only one I had.

Momma spotted me getting out of the car. She rushed out of the house in her bathrobe and embraced me roughly. "Oh, Lil Lil! You're safe. I tried to call you. I called your sister and Ann and even that Thomas guy that Bently told me about. I couldn't even get a hold of the police station to talk to Henry. I so glad you're safe. You're home. Oh, honey…"

On and on, she cried into my hair. I held onto her, shushed her worries, and asked after Marissa and Ann. "They're fine," she answered, wiping her cheeks. "All they had was some wind damage, and we only got some heavy rain."

Bryce moved for the first time, edging around the side of the car, and Momma noticed him. "Mr. King! You're here." She blinked at the simplicity of her words and how confused they sounded.

"Good evening, Mrs. Watson," he replied smoothly. I considered the irony of his polite statement and rolled my eyes. "I am just making sure Lily arrived here safely. Good night."

He returned to the driver's side, giving me a nod. Momma stumbled forward, "Wait!"

He did, placing his point of focus somewhere over both our shoulders. Momma smiled graciously, remembering her manners. "Thank you, Mr. King. For Lily…" I inserted a biting growl for effect. Momma ignored me. "I hope we didn't inconvenience you. Surely, you didn't come all this way to check on Lily."

If there was a hint of a question there, I told myself I was mistaken in hearing it. Then I noticed the car between us. His red Porsche rested in the driveway, the paint chipped in places, the hood battered as though someone took a hammer to it, and a long, nasty scratch graced the whole passenger side. Also, I spied what looked like a piece of a pine bough sticking out of the rear wheel well.

Bryce attempted to answer Momma's suspicious gratitude. I butted in, "Whoa! You *drove* here? Are you crazy? Look at what you did to your car!"

His eyes took in my expression. After a long moment, he shrugged, "It's just a car, Lily. And apparently, I needed to hear you yell at me again, so yes, I drove five hundred miles to get my butt chewed."

"But…you…" I stammered, "you *drove* here! Through hail…and a tornado. Have you absolutely lost your mind? You could have been killed. Have you any

210

idea how bad that would be?"

He laughed softly, "Yes, I do have an idea."

The phone jingled inside the house. Momma hurried through an excuse and rushed to answer it. I could only stare at the man in front of me. My vision glazed over at the images running through my mind. I felt faint, my breath coming in spurts.

"Lily? Are you okay?"

Somehow I ended up on the ground again, with his arms around me…again. "Lily, sweetheart, open your eyes. Talk to me. Do you feel sick?"

A low wail escaped, "But you could have been killed…"

He chuckled and held my head against his chest. The rumbled of his amusement soothed me. "I'm sorry. I had to see you."

"Why?"

"Well, because…I missed you. I love you."

"Oh, Bryce!" I pushed him away. He fell back, resting his arms on his knees. "You should just go home."

He inhaled slowly, and let out the breath with deliberate patience. "Of course, Lily. I will leave you now." He brushed his pants off, towering over me. "I had to take the chance. You left that morning without a good-bye. Then you wouldn't call me back. *Then* you changed all your phone numbers. I guess I blinded myself to what you thought you wanted. Now I know. Thank you for everything we've shared. The memories will always be special to me. As you will be."

He waited for me to say something. What was there

to say? "I missed you, too"? "I love you"? I just didn't have it in me to utter those three words to another man. I didn't have it in myself to allow myself to fall in love with him. With a heavy shrug, he turned.

Momma came bounding out of the house, yelling, "Wait! Mr. King! Wait!" Her eyes were red and puffy. She'd been crying again.

"Momma? What is it? Was that Daddy? Is he okay?"

She hugged me with one arm, "Oh, no dear. Your father is fine, I guess. That was Greta on the phone. It seems Chi Chi ran out into the storm and hasn't returned."

"Wel, I'm sure he'll be fine. He always runs off."

"I know, dear, but your Aunt Greta is worried sick. I'm going over there to sit with her—"

"What? No!" I rounded on her. "Aunt Greta will be alright without you. You need to be here, in case Daddy calls, or Mr. Grayson, or…I…I need you, Momma," I faltered, feeling my own tears well up again.

She secured my body in a motherly hug. "Lil Lil, I'm worried sick about your father, too, but I can't sit here anymore waiting for something to happen. Greta needs me, and I'm going. But don't you worry; you won't be alone." She looked at Bryce over my head, pleading in her face. "I am asking Mr. King if he will stay with you until I get back."

I froze. Momma had a good hold of me, tightening her embrace when she felt my physical protest as though to say, *Shut up, Lily.* I couldn't see Bryce, so I listened for his answer.

"Please, Mr. King," Momma begged again. I could

only imagine the conflict he displayed at her request. "You've been a good friend to this family, and I trust you. Lily trusts you—"

"Don't speak for me," I muttered and felt a sharp pop on my backside. "Ow."

Momma continued, "You can stay in Marissa's old room for the night. I really don't want Lily to be alone."

"I can call Ann," I said.

"Ann has her own problems right now," Momma said in my ear.

The muffled sound of feet shifting pricked my ears, and then Bryce answered her, "Thank you for the offer, Mrs. Watson, but—"

My shoulders slumped with relief, but Momma halted anymore of what he would say. "No, Mr. King," her voice took on that deep tone that always had me cringing with a guilty conscience, even if I was innocent. "I won't hear it. I am not asking anymore. You *will* keep my daughter company tonight."

As a child, I was never able to dispute that voice or the firmness of the decisions it announced. I wondered how Bryce took it. I spared a glance over my shoulder. His eyes held a cornered-rat fear, but a tiny smile graced his mouth.

"It would be my pleasure, Mrs. Watson."

"Good," Momma said, normally, and let me go. "Come in, both of you and get cleaned up. Lily, you're a mess…again."

Bryce followed me slowly as I glared at my mother's back.

~~~~~

He sensed that déjà vu, entering the Watson's home again after so few weeks. But under the circumstances, it was an uncomfortable feeling. Nomi Watson scurried around, gathering an overnight bag and commenting on items in the fridge if they got hungry. Lily pursued her every move, still trying to convince her mother to not go.

But he understood Nomi a little better now. She was soft spoken, like her oldest daughter, but she also expected someone to do as she asked, without argument. Bryce felt that determination in her voice, and he couldn't muster the will to disappoint her.

Finally, Nomi left with a kiss to Lily's cheek and a promise to call when she arrived at her sister's. Bryce said nothing up until that point, but when they were alone, he asked, "So, who – or what – is Chi Chi?"

"Aunt Greta's Pomeranian," Lily answered with a huff. "A yelping, biting, fluff ball of a dog, but he's all Aunt Greta has after Uncle William died." She marched over to the desk in the living room. "I need to call Ann."

Lily flipped through the large yellow phone book. Bryce casually asked, "You don't know your best friend's number?"

Lily's crystallized eyes zeroed on him. "I have her on speed dial on my home phone and cell. I don't need to know her number." Then she bit her lip. "Looks like I have to get another cell phone...*again*." She ran her finger down the listings.

"Why did you change your numbers?"

Her index finger thumped the page, and she picked up the phone without answering, pushing the buttons. After a quick, one-sided conversation that left her frowning, she put down the receiver and turned to him. "Isn't it obvious?"

Bryce stuffed his hands in his pockets and leaned against the back of the couch. "Explain it to me."

Lily held up her fingers, ticking them off as she spoke, "One, you kept calling; two, Thomas kept calling; three, reporters kept calling; four, you continued to call; and five, *you kept calling!*"

Bryce smiled through the hurt of her insinuations about him. "One," he began, "who is Thomas? Two, why were reporters calling you? And three, why did your father not make bail?" He added that last question as it popped into his head.

"Thomas is supposedly a firefighter that can't seem to take a hint. The reporters wanted to know about Nick's death and your involvement, and my involvement with you. And Daddy didn't make bail because his attorney, Mr. Grayson, is out of town until Sunday." Lily brushed past him to stomp to the kitchen.

"Could he not acquire another attorney?" He trailed after her, finding her head stuck in the freezer. She emerged with a gallon of chocolate fudge ice cream and yanked a giant spoon from a drawer.

"No," she snarled. "Daddy only trusts Mr. Grayson. He didn't want anyone else. Otherwise you wouldn't have been forced to stay here, and I wouldn't be having this conversation."

"Okay. Then why won't Mr. Grayson be back until Sunday. Surely, he would return for the sake of a client."

"He's in Fayetteville," Lily said around a mouthful of ice cream. A smudge of chocolate garnished the corner of her bottom lip, and Bryce felt an overwhelming urge to lick it off for her. "It's the first game of the season this weekend," she went on, waving her spoon. "Luke, his son, is the star line backer. He wouldn't miss it for the world, and Daddy knows that."

Bryce blinked at her. "You mean to tell me, your father is locked in a jail cell for the whole weekend because of a football game?"

Lily rolled her eyes. "They're playing Ole Miss. There hasn't been a ticket available for weeks. I don't know how it is in Texas, but around here, the Razorbacks are next to God."

"Are they that good?"

Lily guffawed, spitting ice cream down her chin. "Well, they're not *bad*. We were really good in the eighties with Coach Hatfield, but it's been kind of a roller coaster since then. Good years, bad years...*really* bad years. Still, we hope. Every year."

"I see," Bryce drew out, but he didn't. He let the football excuse pass for the moment and asked, "What evidence did the police have against your father?"

Lily's spoon speared the frozen fudge, and she left it there. Her reply came sadly, "Supposedly, Daddy was the last one to see Nick alive, and his prints were all over Nick's boat. But his boat was still docked, so they think Daddy killed Nick on the lake, pushed his body into the water, and drove his boat back."

"Sounds circumstantial to me," he said. Lily shrugged. "His motive?"

"The house designs and the software program," she pointed to him, "that you now own. Daddy went to see Nick because Nick found out about you buying the company and tried to blackmail Daddy with a copy of the design program, which he somehow got a copyright for. He planned to hold up the sale of the company unless Daddy paid him a quarter of a million dollars, and if that didn't work, Nick said he would come to you with the issue. Nick was just trying to stick his hand in the pot, but Daddy didn't pay him much mind, not after everything else he's tried to pull in the past." Lily grunted. "Good old St. Nick. I'm surprised you didn't know all of this, if Nick really did try to contact you."

"And what does your father say about all that?"

"He's not saying. He knows not to talk until Mr. Grayson comes back." She left the ice cream container on the counter and left the room. "I'm going to take a shower. Marissa's room is the second on the left. Good night."

He watched as she climbed the stairs, her head hung and her feet dragging. This had to be one of the worst days for her. But she was still Lily, fighting mad in a shell of worry and misery. And Bryce loved her all the more for it.

His cell phone jingled in his pocket. "Please tell me you have some good news," he told Justin over the line.

"I don't know if it's good news, but I've just found out the reasons for Watson's arrest."

Bryce inserted, "Fingerprints and the last to see

Garcia alive."

Justin clicked his tongue. "I really hate it when you steal my thunder."

"It's a load of bull, is what it is," Bryce replied fiercely. "Fingerprints aren't exactly damning evidence."

"It's the location of the fingerprints that sealed Watson's arrest," Justin said. "One clear thumb print on the steering wheel of the boat and another on the ignition key."

"That only suggests that he drove the boat," Bryce said, pacing around the dark living room. A gold frame sat above the fireplace. Lily and Marissa, as teenagers, smiled back at him. He picked it up to gaze at it closely. "It does not add up to murder. In fact, it reeks of a badly laid plot. Find out who, or what, would benefit from Henry Watson going to jail, or being accused of murder." He told Justin what Lily had just explained to him.

"We've got a rat in the company," he said, putting the picture back on the mantle.

"Morrissey," Justin answered immediately. "Since all the board members have to be notified of a contract, he could have figured out Garcia's attachment to the Watsons."

"It's more likely that Garcia found out about Morrissey's hatred of me after he got wind of the sale and wanted to use that in his favor," Bryce supplied.

"Either way, a little investigative work and now Morrissey knows every dirty little secret about that family. He's good at that. The newspapers have already gotten wind of our connection with the case, and our stocks have been hit hard. Morrissey wants you to go down with the company. And if my guess is correct, he's found a way to do just that. A business deal involving murder seems like a good way to ruin you. To be honest, I think we should just cut our losses and dissolve that construction company."

Bryce picked up another photo frame, this one taken recently during a golf tournament. He marveled at how happy Lily was. Even with sweat dripping off her temples, she shone with a surreal beauty. Cutting their losses wouldn't really solve this problem, and he couldn't do that to Lily. "Watson Construction remains the way it is for now, but Henry is going to need an attorney."

Justin sighed, resigned, "Doesn't he have one?"

"Yes, but he'll need one that works weekends. Justin, find the best defendant in the city, and do whatever you have to. Lily needs her father home."

"I hope you know what you're doing," Justin said.

"Keep me posted," Bryce returned and hung up.

He found Marissa's bedroom, stripped to his jockeys, and climbed into the pink, flowery bed, all the while suppressing his gag reflex. He lay awake, staring at the ceiling and thinking about how he could help the woman down the hall.

Chapter Seventeen

I took a deep breath and couldn't believe what I was about to do. Bryce King came back for me, and that had to mean something. The realization hit me as the hot shower washed away the dirt and soreness. He would do this for me. Or he might not. My family, and my father's life, was at stake. Using his feelings for me against him wasn't my best moment, but I had to try.

I knocked on the bedroom door. "Bryce, are you awake?" I whispered and pushed the door open. He sat up in Marissa's silly girlish bed, and I stifled the giggle. He looked so uncomfortable.

"I'm awake," he said. I came into the room and perched on the side of the mattress.

"Listen, I'm sorry for acting like such an unworthy jerk tonight," I began, swallowing the lump in my throat. I focused on his face, trying my hardest to ignore his bare chest in the early morning light coming through the window. "I've had a rough day, and you didn't deserve any of it."

"What is it you want, Lily?" he asked sharply.

"I'm, um, well, did you mean what you said?"

"Which part?"

"That you missed me?" I'd almost asked if he meant that he loved me, but I couldn't. I felt guilty about what I was about to do.

His eyes softened, and he reached over to cover my hand. "Yes, Lily. I've missed you."

My untouched fingers fiddled with the neckline of the nightgown I'd chosen for initiating my plan. It was a sheer black, lacy thing that dipped down between my breasts, and I knew he noticed from the way he kept darting glances at it. I took another deep breath and closed my eyes.

Get on with it, Lily!

"I'm offering myself to you," I said, blowing out the breath in a rush.

"I beg your pardon?"

My hand under his gentle caress clenched in a fist at those words. *Really?* However, I let it pass and remembered my proposal. "I want you to get Daddy out of this. I'll do anything you want. Be anything you want. *Anything.* But please, do this for me. I don't care what it takes. You have the money and the power and the connections. You can do it. I know you can. I'll be your mistress, be at your beck and call twenty-four, seven, fix your plumbing, build you a bigger tree house for your nephews, teach your sister to cook, and have your children. Whatever you want from me. I don't care. I'll do it. I want my father back. I want my family back together."

His touch withdrew as I babbled, tears streaming down my cheeks. I got to the point where I couldn't look at him from the shame of what I was offering, but I *didn't* care. Daddy was the world to me. I meant what I said. I would do anything it took.

I had what Bryce wanted; he could do what I wanted. The strange thing was, I actually wanted to do what he asked anyway. He didn't need to know that, and I wasn't going to bring it up.

The minutes stretched. Only the chirping of early birds filled the silence. I risked a glance. Astonishment could not even describe his expression.

"Please, Bryce." I left it at that and waited.

~~~~~

She's kidding, right? She's distraught and tired and confused, and she couldn't really be prostituting herself to free her father. Could she?

"Lily," he whimpered and cleared his throat, "I think you need to get some sleep and think about what you are asking me."

She clamped her hands together and sighed. "I know what I'm doing. This isn't exhaustion speaking. It's in earnest. I mean every word."

Bryce shook his head. "No, Lily. I won't do it."

Her head snapped up, fire forming behind the dampness of her tears. But she held her temper in check and Bryce watched the control with fascination. She really was serious about this. Then he watched as she edged closer to him, pulling at the ribbons that kept that indecently sexy nightgown from falling from her shoulders. Her breasts bared themselves, and he fought for every breath.

Lily leaned in, the black lace falling to a puddle around her waist. "I can make you change your mind," she rasped.

He pressed into the lacy pillows behind his back, trying to flee the temptation before him. Short of jumping out of the bed and giving her a glimpse of just how aroused he was, he had nowhere to run.

"Lily, you're playing with fire here. I won't let you

do this."

She hitched her knees onto the mattress beside him and threw one leg over, pinning him. "If this is what it takes, Bryce, I'm afraid you can't stop me." She placed a hand on either side of his head and swept her tongue over his lips. He grabbed a fistful of sheet in either hand to anchor them away from her body.

"Lily, don't do this to me," he begged.

"I know you want me," she murmured, settling on top of him. "I can feel you." She kissed him softly once, then twice, mere tingling brushes that left him dizzy. She sucked his bottom lip into her sweet mouth and nibbled.

"Please don't," he tried again.

"Anything you want," she said.

"Not like this."

"Love me, Bryce," she commanded with her mouth. "Love me like you say you do."

Even the sheets couldn't keep his hands off her then. There was only so much restraint in his body. He sat straight up, lashing his tongue against hers, lacing his fingers through her damp hair as her legs maneuvered to lock around his waist. With an acrobatic feat, he flipped her over and took all she had to offer.

Hours later, Lily snuggled next to him with a happy smile. He traced that contented curve with his thumb. She opened it to bite down gently, and then sucked the small pain away.

"You have a phenomenon mouth, Lily," he moaned. "It's very talented."

"Thank you," she said. "I could say the same about

yours."

"Could?" he asked, arching an eyebrow.

"Well, I don't want to disgrace you with such an understated description." Lily raised her head to kiss him. He lingered there, feeling his body respond wearily in protest at his arousal.

"You have to stop that," he said. "You're wearing me out."

"I'm wearing you *down*," she boasted.

"For your information, I was already prepared to do all I could to help your father."

She drew back a little to look squarely at him. "You mean...why didn't you say something earlier?"

She was too far away from him; he tugged her into his arms again. "I tried, and then you distracted me. If you had just asked me, instead of trying to seduce me first, you would have known that."

"*Tried* to seduce you? I believe I did a pretty damn good job of that," she replied.

He chuckled into her hair. "Lily, you never have to try. I'll take everything you have to offer. In any way you wish to give it. But you see now, you have created your own worst nightmare. You will *never* get rid of me after this stunt of yours. I promise you that I meant those three little words. I love you, and I'll do anything for you. You have me for life. And that is not just a promise; it's a threat."

Lily chewed that over as she bit the side of her lip. She narrowed her eyes up at him. "Does that mean I can have you again?"

"Don't you ever get tired?"

"I'm dog-tired," she admitted. "But that has never slowed me down."

"Hmm," he mused, pressing his mouth on hers. She melted against him and grinned with clear victory. When he withdrew, she whimpered. He whispered hotly on her cheek, "I hear your mother downstairs."

Lily jerked up so fast, she bumped her head on his nose. "Oh, no," she cried. "Momma will kill me if she sees us. She'll kill you, too."

She scrambled out of the bed, taking the blanket to hide her naked body and fled the room. Bryce threw himself back into the mattress and grinned.

"I love you, Lily Watson," he said to the room.

"Well, that's good to know," Nomi Watson said from the open door. Bryce's heart leapt out of his chest when he saw her. "Because otherwise, seeing my daughter running down the hall, practically naked, would give me cause to find Henry's shotgun."

She put her hands on her hips and glanced at him. "But as it is, Lily is old enough to make her own decisions, and far too old to not give me five little grandchildren I can spoil." She smiled smugly at him. "You two will have beautiful children. Get dressed, Mr. King. I'll make you some breakfast."

~~~~~

"This is not good," Bryce said into the phone. Justin sent him a list of lawyers willing to take Watson's case, and the name of the prosecutor and presiding judge. "Why do those names sound familiar? Erickson and

Porterhouse?"

"Because they're both in Morrissey's pocket," Justin explained. "And Prescott, our investigator, learned something else. Morrissey's right hand man, Hall, has not been seen in months. Then all of a sudden he pops up on the radar. He's living in Little Rock, Bryce, under a different name."

"Retired, or working for Morrissey?"

"Prescott's looking into it," Justin said. "My gut tells me he's working."

"I'm getting the same vibe," Bryce said. "See if Prescott has connections in Little Rock and have Hall followed. I don't want him anywhere near Lily."

"And, speaking of Morrissey, he wants a meeting with you. Shall I have Gloria set up a time?"

"Sometime next week," Bryce agreed, wondering what the old man had up his sleeve now.

~~~~~

Daddy was able to make bail on Monday morning, and Mr. Grayson was only too pleased to have the assistance of the best attorneys that the surrounding states could offer and Bryce's money could buy. Between the four lawyers, Daddy got to stay at home, although his trial would take place in Dallas, and he was granted a rushed trial date.

"Circumstantial evidence," Mr. Grayson kept saying. "The prosecuting attorney, Joel Erickson, is still young and looking for a promotion. He wasn't aware of what he was getting himself into when he went after Mr.

226

Watson. Don't worry about it, Lily. They only have the barest of evidence to charge your father. We'll find ways to throw most of that out of court."

And as it turned out, Mr. Grayson was correct. The evidence was shady, but so was the prosecutor. He continued to offer explanations for the misconstrued data, so much so that the judge allowed most of it to stay. The only fingerprints found that belonged to Daddy were the two that sealed his arrest. No others were found, not even smudged or even belonging to Nick. But Prosecutor Erickson had an excuse for that. Nick's boat had a spark-plug problem and didn't start, so it obviously could not have been used in his murder, but Erickson found out that the problem was a recent issue for the boat and could have been planted after use. On and on, the two sides parried. I got dizzy just thinking about it and tried to divert my attention elsewhere.

So, I spent most my next few weeks running Daddy's company while he took some leave time, meeting with lawyers and trying to clean up the mess I once called a house. The entire pin oak had to be chopped and sawed away before I could rummage through the ruins for anything worth saving. I managed to fill up a small moving van with items, but the pile of discards inside the giant dumpster was larger by far.

At work, the employees began the final stages of the development. Every lot had a structure, of one stage or another, and a couple houses were ready for their first ever occupants. By mid October, the neighborhood would be completely finished, and Daddy's retirement – if he wasn't convicted – would begin.

And if I didn't have enough problems, evading Fireman Thomas became part of my everyday routine. He showed up one day at the work site to speak briefly with Bently, and to ask me out on a date. I said, "No. I'm busy that night." He popped around the canned foods aisle at the grocery store and asked if I wanted to go to a movie that night. I said, "No, I'm having dinner at my parents tonight." He happened to be in the neighborhood one afternoon while I was hauling damaged furniture out of my home and asked if I needed any help. I said, "No, I'm finished for the day." And then he asked if he could drive me back to my parent's house.

Everyday, it was something. And everyday, I grew more and more jumpy, thinking the blonde idiot was about to stick his head out of the water cooler and say, "So how about dinner tonight?" or fall from the sky and offer to help me lay tar paper on site three's roof.

Finally, after literally bumping into him at the hardware store, I asked, "Are you stalking me?"

He shrugged, grinned lazily, and said, "I like you. I think we should see more of each other."

In my hand, I gripped a new pry bar and a box of drywall screws. I jammed the pry bar under Thomas' jugular and said, "I'll only tell you this one more time. I'm seeing someone else. I have no interest in you, I do not like you, and I have no desire to date you. And if I ever find out that you are following me, I'll shove more than a pry bar up your nose. Are we clear?"

He swallowed, nodded, sneered, and backed away. I haven't seen hide nor hair of him since. Of course, that left me with one little problem: Bryce King.

I'd fallen recklessly in love with a multimillionaire who couldn't tell the difference between a miter saw and a belt grinder. I couldn't help it, and I couldn't stop it. One day, I was gently prying the only unbroken stained glass window in my house when he cupped his hands over my eyes, whispered, "Guess who?" and took me up against the wall in my dining room. I grumped that I was sweaty and covered in dust and hadn't shaved my legs in three days, and he just kissed me and said, "I love it when you talk dirty," and made love to me again on the paint tarp by the boarded-up window.

And he continued to claim that he loved me, a woman with sawdust in her hair and mud up to her knees. Somewhere, someone had kidnapped Cupid and screwed up all his pairings because Lily Watson and Bryce King made the most unsuited couple since God mixed a duck with a beaver and created the platypus. Every time I saw the man, I couldn't breathe without the air catching painfully in my throat and my stomach tying into knots. At first, I assumed I had a bad case of indigestion. Nope.

Love.

After my disastrous marriage with Nick, I swore to myself I'd never fall for another suit-and-tie man. And I would never, never, ever make myself ill for not being with him. I wasn't a lovesick teenager, by any means. However, those long stretches of time when I wandered through my days alone, I found myself not wanting to eat or sleep, and then I would oversleep by several hours and stuff myself with fried peanut butter sandwiches and summer sausage.

So, yes, I, lily Watson of Little Rock, Arkansas, fell frantically in love with Bryce King, and I was so happy and content with the idea...so at peace with my acknowledgment.

But for the life of me, I couldn't figure out why I wanted to throw up whenever I thought of him.

~~~~~

"Mr. Morrissey," Bryce said, rising from his desk to meet the man. "I'll forgo the pleasantries, considering how you're trying to rip my company out from under me."

"And you must forgive me for not shaking your hand," Benjamin Morrissey stated, "considering how you were responsible for my wife's death."

Bryce sighed. "I do wish you could be reasonable about that. If I had taken up Charlotte's offer, you would still feel animosity toward me."

"Then we are at an impasse," Morrissey said.

"Maybe you can explain why you feel the need to ruin the life of an innocent man," Bryce suggested.

"I'm afraid I don't know what you're talking about," the older man returned.

"Yes, I'm sure you don't. Henry Watson did not kill Nicolas Garcia. You know that as well as I do."

"I only know what I read in the papers," Morrissey said, examining a photo of Lily on his desk. "New girlfriend?"

"No," Bryce said, taking the picture frame away from him. "The only girlfriend."

"So, it is true. You are involved with Watson's daughter. That is interesting. First, the company is tied to a murder, and now the CEO is dating the ex-wife of the deceased. Sounds like one of those soap operas that Vivian likes to watch. My task shall be easier than I thought."

"And what task would that be?" Bryce asked, tucking Lily's photo away in a drawer.

"To destroy you, of course," Morrissey answered calmly, looking Bryce square in the eye. Bryce stared back, keeping eye contact. The man refused to see reason. Morrissey was old enough that maybe Bryce could use dementia or the early stages of Alzheimer's against him, if necessary. Benjamin Morrissey would not get his hands on King Enterprises.

"Why is Hall in Arkansas?" Bryce inquired suddenly.

Morrissey hitched a shoulder and crossed an ankle over the other knee. "Thomas is taking an extended vacation. I don't know where he is at the moment."

"Are you claiming that your stooge happens to be in the same city as the Watsons out of coincidence?"

Morrissey shrugged again, but didn't answer.

Bryce stood, a clear indication that he was finished with this meeting. "I don't know what hand you're playing. But you need to leave Lily and her family out of this. Your issue is with me. I'd prefer to keep it that way. Otherwise..."

"Yes?" Morrissey raised an eyebrow. "Otherwise,

what?"

"Otherwise, I will be the least of your problems," Bryce finished. Morrissey considered that, nodded with acceptance, and left without another word. Bryce was dialing Justin's office before the door closed. "Justin, who do we know at the courthouse?"

"Janet Simpson," he answered, "why?" A half second later, Justin groaned and added, "Lily won't like it."

"She already told me to do whatever it took," Bryce returned, cringing at the thought of telling Lily that he was resorting to bribery. That woman had an uncanny sense of right and wrong. Lying, cheating, and corruption were all great and dandy, as long as they helped clear her father's name. Otherwise, he couldn't imagine the fury of her anger.

"Fine," Justin resigned, "who do you want gone, the judge or the prosecutor?"

"Which ever is easiest and less likely to draw suspicion."

Chapter Eighteen

"You did WHAT?!"

Bryce sighed and flipped over to his back. He probably thought that one of our lovemaking sessions would be the best way to approach this subject. I scrambled off my bed and paced the floor, naked. It was the middle of the day. Luckily, both Momma and Daddy weren't home.

"Why am I not surprised?" I asked, stopping to glare at him for effect. "I know I told you that I would do anything, but not blackmail. Not to a judge. And definitely not when Grayson swears that Daddy won't be convicted."

"Lily..."

"No, don't you Lily me," I hissed at him. "This is wrong. Why can't you see that you can't use your power and money that way?"

Bryce sat upright and declared, "I spend roughly nine million dollars annually on charities around the world. I think that a little credit is due, Lily. I'm not a selfish bastard, and I do what I can to help those in need. And your father needs this. That judge was in Morrissey's back pocket. There was no way Henry would have been acquitted, even with the shoddy evidence."

"What are you talking about? Who the hell is Morrissey?"

Bryce hopped out of the bed and tugged on his jeans. "Benjamin Morrissey is the man responsible for Garcia's death. And for framing Henry. All of this is because Morrissey feels I was responsible for his wife's suicide three years ago."

"Were you?"

He gave me an even stare. "Of course not."

I slumped on a beanbag in the corner. My bedroom in my parent's house still looked like it did when I left it ten years ago to attend college out of state. I really needed to find my own place. Living here while I repaired my house was not the best of ideas. Especially when that included finding opportunities to sneak Bryce up the stairs. "This sounds like a bad *Law And Order* episode," I mumbled. "Can we prove that this Morrissey guy killed Nick?"

"I'm working on it," Bryce said, his voice muffled through the shirt he was pulling over his head. I pursed my lips at him. He had a habit of getting dressed in the middle of sex. "What are you doing?"

"Having a serious conversation," he replied, smiling gently. "You know that's impossible for me when we're both naked. Would you put on something, please?"

I ignored that request. "How exactly did all this happen? Why Nick? Why Daddy?"

Bryce tossed a blanket in my direction, which I threw down on the floor. He breathed an exasperated huff and leaned against the bedposts, keeping his eyes on my face. Then he told me a story. Charlotte Morrissey, the suicidal wife, approached Bryce with several sexual propositions a few years ago. Bryce turned her down, and the woman, being unstable to begin with, killed herself, thinking she was undesirable. Benjamin Morrissey blamed Bryce. I snorted, "Would he have been happy if you slept with her?"

Bryce agreed with my sentiments and continued, "The reason I bought Watson Construction was because an associate of mine, Vivian Corter, wanted to sell her shares in another company, but would only sell to me if I agreed to help your father out. I thought she was being charitable, helping out an old friend. Then I found out that she had eloped with Morrissey, and several pieces fell together.

"Somehow, Garcia found out about Morrissey's vendetta against me, wanted to make some quick cash, and sought out Morrissey with this plan to ruin me through my business transactions. Garcia had a copy of your original home designs and that blueprint software, right? Since the software isn't open to the public yet, it wouldn't be difficult to fake a copyright to it. I'm guessing that Morrissey found out that Garcia was lying about his rights to the plans so he had him killed, planted evidence that would lead to your father, and had a judge and a prosecutor assigned who would do anything Morrissey asks."

I frowned at the floor. This kind of thing doesn't happen to normal people. Nick was killed because some rich dude held a grudge? "Can we prove any of that?"

"Not a single fact," Bryce said quietly, "but that doesn't mean I'm giving up. Your life has been turned upside down because of me. I'm not proud of that, and I can only hope that someday you will forgive me."

I looked up at him. Gracious, it should be a mortal sin to fall in love with men like him. Cool, confident, gorgeous, sweet, and wealthy. "I think you're gonna have to beg me for forgiveness," I said in my best come-hither voice.

He grinned, advanced with predatory steps, and then groaned with annoyance when Momma called, "Lil Lil! We're home!"

"That's it," he said, searching for his shoes while I hurried to throw some clothes on. "I'm getting you your own place to live in. I haven't snuck out of a girl's window since high school."

Good to his word, Bryce bought a house in my neighborhood for me to live in while mine was being repaired. He racked up some considerable air miles with all the trips back and forth between Arkansas and Dallas as well. He worked for a few days, flew to Little Rock for a day, made love to me all night, and then flew back. This pattern repeated well into September. And every time, I had to say something.

"Bryce, you can't keep doing this," I said after one very long erotic session of heart-pounding sex that christened my new dining room table.

"I can do this all night," he replied, licking down my neck and rubbing a thumb over my exposed breast.

"No," I laughed, "I meant you flying back and forth."

"If you'd just move in with me in Dallas, I wouldn't have to fly back and forth," he pointed out against my throat.

"I work here," I reminded him. "Speaking of which, how are you getting any work done? Or sleep, for that matter. You send me twenty emails a day and you call me just as often. And you're getting thinner. I'm going to have a talk with Maria."

"Maria feeds me. I eat, I promise you." His tongue found that breast and his thumb moved on to softer, wetter places.

I giggled, "Funny that you should say it that way. Especially here, on my new table."

"This is a very nice table," he commented. "And I really like the new couch. Much better than that green monster you had. This one looks inviting."

I slapped him on the shoulder. "You're changing the subject."

"You did that. I'm just keeping up with your topics." He scooted down and hauled me up and around his waist. Carrying me across the room and through the adjoining door, his mouth ravished mine, slipping his tongue in and out. We fell together over the back of the couch.

"Like I was saying," I tried again as his fingers played with the skin over my belly and ribcage. "This can't be good for you. You're missing a lot of work being here, and people are beginning to talk."

His mouth nuzzled under my ear and he asked, "Which people?"

"Well, everyone I work with, for one. You popped in out of the blue last week, remember? I'm still being harassed about the 'Shaking Shack.'"

He chortled as his lips traveled down my neck and across my collarbone. "'Shaking Shack.' I like that one. I like this couch, too. It's very wide. We haven't made love on the couch yet, have we?"

"You can't be serious," I groaned. "I have to get up in the morning. It's already after midnight. I think twice today is enough."

As his thumb found – according to him – the gateway to Eden, my body arched up of its own accord. His index finger glided into me, rubbing the small mound of flesh just inside the opening.

"Mmm, that feels good," I moaned.

"That's why I do it. Did I mention I really like this couch?"

"Quit distracting me…oh! Okay, distract me."

And that was our pattern. The couch was the last piece of furniture in my new, temporary home to lay claim to our time together, but my bed, my shower, my staircase, and many, many other areas received just as much attention. Bryce flew back to Dallas a week before Daddy's trial, and two days later, I found out I wasn't sick in love with Bryce.

I was pregnant.

Oh, I still loved that unflappable and composed man. But the lovesick indigestion I thought I had turned out to be a new life. And I was terrified. Bryce didn't know. Since we'd been together, he clammed up tight whenever Momma or Daddy brought up grandchildren. He really didn't want to have any. And I didn't know what to do about that. And when I worried about Bryce's reaction, I either ate more or threw up more, or both, and that was getting old very quickly. He'd already told me that he didn't want children. His irrational fear of having an autistic child seemed to commandeer my thoughts most of the day. What if he tells me to abort it? What if he decides that he doesn't want to be with me anymore? What if he thinks I tricked him into a family? He always teased me about that, calling me "Daisy" and the one time I asked him about it, he grumbled something about "barefoot and pregnant" and I didn't push it.

Then I'd have moments of endearing sweetness. I'm having a baby! Bryce's baby. I hoped for a son that looked just like his father, and I hoped for a girl that would hold her daddy's heart in her fist, and I hoped for twins so that I could have one of each. Bryce would be a wonderful father, as devoted to his child as he was to everything else, and I would sit under my shade tree at work, rubbing my belly and smiling, and thinking about the years ahead of us. The three of us playing golf together, taking trips, building a tree house of our own.

That week, Bryce flew to Seattle for business, and I didn't have the guts to tell him over the phone. So for five days, I fretted. I tried talking to Ann, but as it turned out, she was pregnant, too, and so vibrant over the idea of her first child, that I didn't want to spoil her happiness. Marissa was no help because pregnancy was a sore spot with her, and when I got the nerve to tell Momma and Daddy, all they could think about was redecorating my bedroom into a nursery for their new grandchild.

That was my life for five long days. A rollercoaster of emotions and worries, happiness and anxiety. When Daddy's trial day arrived, I saw Bryce for the first time since I'd stared wide-eyed at the plus sign on the pregnancy test. He hired a private jet to fly the whole family to Dallas and granted his guesthouse for their use.

No one said anything about my own accommodations, which included a special place along side Bryce in his own bedroom. I warned them to keep their mouths shut until I had a chance to talk to him, but from the way Daddy heartily embraced Bryce's handshake and from Momma's tearful hug and smothering cheek kisses, he had to suspect something.

"Either your parents are particularly optimistic about tomorrow's trial, or there is something else going on that I don't know about." He slid into his bed beside me, pulling me into the crook of his arm.

"I think that maybe it's a little of both," I muttered with some anxiety. His hand slithered under the hem of my nightshirt, warming the skin of my belly and caressing the curve under my breast. His mouth nuzzled behind my ear, and he sighed, "I've missed you. I nearly ravished you in the airport."

"I missed you, too," I replied, a little more stiffly than I should have. He shied away from me.

"So, there is something else?"

"Bryce," I said, laying my palm against his jaw and tilting his face up to look at me. "There's something I should tell you. But first, I want you to know that you are possibly the greatest thing that has ever happened to me, despite all that has gone on since we've met."

He kissed my palm and smiled, but a lot of wary filled his expression. "If you're going to tell me that you love me, I already know."

"No, that's not it," I said.

"So you don't love me," he teased.

"Oh," I frowned, "well, actually what I have to say is

a little more important than that."

"What is more important than love?" He winked and bent down to drink from my mouth.

"Um...I'm pregnant?"

Whatever he had in mind to do next, it never happened. All movement ceased, even his breathing. Shock smothered his face, and my worst fear was confirming in my heart. I felt bile rise. If he loved me, it was not enough for something like this.

"I beg your pardon?"

"I'm pregnant," I said a little more solidly. "Five weeks, by my guess. Which places the time of conception on the morning after that storm. And considering how careful we've been since then..."

He propped up on his elbow to stare into my eyes. "You're sure?"

"It was the only time without a condom, and you've been the only man in my life in the last year. And I took three home tests, all positive. I'm sure."

"And your plan?"

I blinked stupidly at him. "My plan? Really, Bryce?"

"I need to know."

I threw a robe over my shoulders and put as much space between us as possible. Which meant escaping to his balcony and inhaling lungfuls of cool night air. How can he be so obtuse? So cold? It was a baby, not an invoice!

"Lily," Bryce said, coming up behind me. "I'm sorry. But I need to know how you feel about this."

"This is good news," I uttered, not looking at him. "My parents will finally have their own grandchild."

"But what about you, Lily?"

"Well...I'm happy, Bryce. Your child is growing in my body, and I want it." I turned and leaned against the railing, facing him with determination, sticking my chin in the air. "I'm keeping this baby, whether you want me to or not. I've never wanted anything more in my life."

"More than me?"

"Yes, Bryce, more than you."

He walked to me, gently putting his hands against my heart. "Is there any room in there for me?"

"There's always room for you, Bryce. I do love you. But if my life with this baby won't include you, then I will be fine with that. At least I will always have a piece of you with me."

"You would willingly have a baby even without a father?"

I shook my head. "No, I would have *your* baby even without its father." And then I realized what that sounded like. "Don't get me wrong," I rushed to fill in. "I'm not asking for anything. I told you once that I didn't want your money. That's still true. I will only take you with your baby or just your baby. I don't want any other combination. And I know you're worried about whether this child with be...different, but I don't care. I won't care if it comes out with three eyes and purple horns. It's my baby, and I'm keeping it."

He blinked at me. "Is that what's been bothering you? That I don't want children because of the possibility of autism?"

I turned away from him. "You said so yourself."

"That was before I fell in love with you and learned

242

that the woman that owns my heart is also carrying my child. I won't care if it has three eyes, purple horns, iridescent scales *and* autism. That's our child. You're my wife--"

"What? We're not married," I said as I whirled around and narrowed my eyes at him. "What did you do?"

He shrugged, "Nothing illegal, I promise you."

I crossed my arms and huffed. "Then what are you talking about? You've never even brought this up in a conversation."

"Our conversations have been limited," he admitted with a smile. I pressed back a grin.

"I rather enjoyed our lack of conversations."

"And I think we should have many, many more years of neglected conversations," he added. "Especially when we're married."

"You didn't ask me to marry you."

"I thought it was obvious."

I pointed at him. "You have to ask, or it's no go."

He smiled and kissed me. "Actually, I thought I'd just give you the ring and let you make the decision."

I tilted back. "I beg your pardon?"

~~~~~

Bryce threw back his head and laughed. "Stay right there," he told me, disappearing into his room. A few seconds later, he came back, now wearing his own robe.

"I had this great evening planned for after the trial, the two of us on the ninth hole at the club, feeding each other pieces of fruit, drinking champagne, making love." He opened a tiny box and presented a simple gold band with the words *Lily, will you marry me?* inscribed around the outside.

He shrugged, "I figured that you wouldn't want a huge four carat diamond on your finger, with it catching on everything while you work..." He stopped speaking as I took the band from the box and gazed at it.

He was right. This was perfect.

"But I can change it," he offered in a hurry when I didn't speak.

"No," I whispered hoarsely.

He exhaled, and it seemed as though he deflated in front of me. "Does that mean you won't marry me?"

I glanced at him, smiling. "No, Bryce. That means don't you dare change this ring. It's perfect just the way it is."

"So, that means you will marry me?"

I hitched a shoulder, "I'm still thinking about it."

Bryce apparently did not appreciate my teasing. He snatched the ring from my fingers and slid it exactly where it should be and will always stay. "No thinking about it," he said in a strong replica of my mother's firm tone. "You will marry me, or I will haul your cute butt down to your parents. I'm sure Nomi will provide a shotgun wedding. She wants grandchildren, and I'm going to give her plenty to keep herself busy. And that goes the same for you."

He kissed my ring finger and jerked his head in a nod.

"Do I not get a say in this?"

"No," he grinned. I held my hand up to the moonlight, loving the way the inscription danced along the gold.

"Momma and Daddy will think you are cheap. No diamond," I commented.

"Got it covered," he said. He lowered a thin platinum chain over my head and around my neck. An ice-blue, diamond pendant the size of my thumbnail hovered in the air and then settled coolly against my skin. "I couldn't just *not* get you a diamond, but I thought this was more your style."

He stepped back to admire his handiwork and smiled victoriously. "The same color as your eyes," he murmured. "I was afraid it would be too dark."

"It's beautiful."

"As well it should be. I had it made for you. My jeweler got rather perturbed with me. I had to send back the first two. They weren't the right shade of blue."

I closed my eyes and forced myself not to consider what he just said. He had a jeweler. Which meant he once bought jewelry for other people, probably other women. *Don't even think about it, Lily.*

"Well, that takes care of the blue," I said more calmly than I felt. "What about the old, the new, and the borrowed?"

He pulled me into his arms and kissed me solidly. "That is your problem, and you have three day's to fix it."

"What?"

"That's the waiting period in Texas. Three days. By this weekend, you will be Mrs. Lily King."

I crossed my arms again and huffed at him...again. This was becoming a habit. As was his take-charge attitude. I kind of liked it, but don't tell him that. "A little say-so will be nice for me. Do I get to make any of the decisions?"

"Absolutely," he said, and pressed a finger to my lips when I opened to speak, "Except the timing. If you want a big wedding, then we can do that at a later date. After the trial tomorrow, we will register for a marriage license and you have seventy-two hours to make all the plans you wish."

"Did you ever consider that I might *want* a long engagement?"

"You're pregnant, and your father owns a shotgun," he pointed out. "We marry this week." I popped my jaw open and snapped it closed, crinkling my brow. "How do you know Daddy owns a shotgun?"

He grinned, lopsided, and said, "Your mother told me, after she caught you escaping Marissa's room that one morning."

"Oh, my God! She knew? Is that why she made you blueberry pancakes?"

"I guess," he shrugged. "Is that significant?"

"She only makes them for special occasions. Birthdays, anniversaries, good report cards...the possibility of grandchildren." I curved my lips secretly. Momma knew about us all along, and she never said anything. That shrew!

"Can we get back to us?" he asked, placing a hand on my belly. "All three of us."

I covered his hand with my own. "Are you sure

about this? I know you're scared about your child having Asperger's. I don't want you to do anything you don't want to do."

"Lil Lil," he muttered, pulling me close. "I love you, and this baby, anyway I can have you."

After a long, torturous kiss that edged my body towards his bed, I slapped him on the shoulder. "You can't call me Lil Lil."

"Just give me a few minutes, and you won't care what I call you," he promised, and he was right.

Chapter Nineteen

Daddy got "lucky." The previous judge came down with "pneumonia", and his new judge threw the case out of court after only two hours. She gave the young prosecutor a lashing about wasting precious resources on crappy evidence and motives.

I almost felt sorry for the guy, but he did try to tear apart my family, and my remorse only lasted until we were driving away from the courthouse and the mulling reporters. But instead of returning to the mansion, Bryce diverted all of us to the marriage office, and my whole family witnessed the beginnings of my future shackles.

The next day, Bryce left early for the office and Momma and Daddy drove out to Aunt Gracie's. Maria spent most of the afternoon shopping for the wedding on Saturday, and I was all alone, with only my bag of clubs and an endless supply of balls. Heaven. Pure Heaven.

After a few hours, and getting a tiny bit lonely and hungry, I left a message on the main house's phone to see if Maria had arrived home.

"You must be Lily Watson," a man's voice said behind me. I whirled around, holding my nine iron like a baseball bat. A balding man with a really sad comb-over smiled pleasantly at me.

"Who are you?"

The man unbuttoned his suit jacket and sat down in one of the club chairs. "I must beg your pardon for intruding, but I felt it necessary to introduce myself. I'm

Benjamin Morrissey."

The blood drained from my head so fast, I felt dizzy.

"I see Mr. King has been keeping you informed," he said calmly and waved at another man behind him. "Have you met my associate, Thomas Hall?"

~~~~~

Bryce couldn't help it. The itch between his shoulder blades refused to go away. His stomach felt full of butterflies, and he just couldn't shake that feeling, like someone was staring at the back of his head. That morning, he languidly kissed Lily good-bye and promised to be home by four o'clock for an early dinner and to help with the wedding preparations. But as soon as he stepped into Gloria's outer office, he stopped, spun around and got that eerie sensation.

"Are you okay, Mr. King?" Gloria asked for the fifth time that day as she walked across the carpet and dropped a package on his desk. "You seem jumpy."

"Did Lily call?"

"No, Mr. King. Would you like for me to try her at home?"

A weird, metallic taste entered his mouth. "Yes, try all the numbers, and the cell numbers as well. Something doesn't feel right."

"I'll let you know as soon as I get a hold of her," she said over her shoulder as she walked out again.

Bryce fidgeted, rearranged the items on his desk, paced the floor, stared out the window at the Dallas sunshine, and eventually gave in to the anxiety.

"Gloria!" he called, gathering his briefcase and suit jacket from the closet.

"Yes, Mr. King?"

"I'm leaving for the day," he told her. "But keep trying Lily. Something doesn't feel right."

"I can have a policeman go by the house, if you want?" she offered, hearing the unease in his words.

"No," he declined. "No sense in involving the police. Lily would have my hide if she saw one more cop." Not to mention the security guard keeping an eye on his house secretly, Bryce thought to himself. Gloria chuckled and picked up the phone to dial the next number. Bryce hurried down the hall and into the elevator. On the way to his car in the parking garage, his cell rang.

"Bryce, where you going?" Justin asked frantically.

"Home."

"Good," his friend said. "Hurry. Prescott just told me that he'd lost Morrissey's trail. And the guard at your place isn't answering his phone. And he thinks Hall is with him."

Bryce clicked off he call and shifted his car down a gear. It would take him twenty minutes to get home, without any downtown traffic. He pulled into his drive at the eighteen-minute mark. "Lily!" he shouted, bursting through the front door.

Maria came rushing forward. "She's out at the clubhouse."

"You know this for sure?"

"She called just a few minutes ago," Maria said.

Bryce took the first full breath of the day. His heart

slowed and relief washed over him in a calming wave. She was okay. Nothing wrong at all. Stepping out the back door, he slowly made his way across his property to the driving range, allowing the extra time for additional soothing breaths.

~~~~~

"Thomas," I sneered at the blonde idiot holding a gun to my head. "Just wait until I tell Bently about this. I'll be able to hijack Movie Night for the next ten years."

"Shut up," Thomas growled and tugged me into the clubhouse. Morrissey followed.

"Don't hurt her, Thomas," the older man said. "We just want to talk."

I made a huge production of sucking snot into my throat, and spat the whole wad on grandpa's shiny black shoe and silently thanked the mongrel brothers for teaching me that trick.

"Ah, yes," Morrissey sighed, eying his soiled loafer. "The unusual manners of hillbillies. Charming."

Thomas threw me crosswise over the back of a chair and told me to stay. "What do you want to talk about?" I asked. "Ooh, I know! How about you explain why you killed my ex-husband? Or about why you tried to ruin my father's life - or, how about how you couldn't keep your wife happy, and she went looking for love somewhere else, which resulted in a night of pill-popping and too much champagne?"

Morrissey's eyes narrowed to mere slits. "Young lady, I suggest that you keep my wife out of this."

"Please," I snorted, sitting upright and pushing the hair out of my face. "If it weren't for your wife, none of us would be here right now."

Just keep him talking, I told myself. And try not to make him mad, which was very, very, very difficult to do. I scanned the room, looking for a weapon I could shove up Thomas' nose and Morrissey's backside. Just keep them talking, and maybe I can get out of this with my skin still intact.

~~~~~

Voices sounded from inside the clubhouse. And Lily's laughter. Bryce approached the nearest door and smiled to himself. He absolutely loved the chime of her laugh. Wondering if her parents were back early, he turned the knob and stepped out of the blistering sun.

The sight before him caused a small heart attack. Lily, hair mussed and sporting fresh bruises, sprawled in one of the leather club chairs. She was laughing, but cynically. Standing before her, in a gray pinstrip suit, was Morrissey.

"Mr. King," he said, "how kind of you to join our little party."

Lily's eyes darted to Bryce's left and pain exploded in his head. Blackness followed.

~~~~~

"Are you crazy?! You could have killed him!"

Bryce crumpled against Thomas, pushing the taller

man away from the open doorway. Running for my life never crossed my mind. I launched across the room to Bryce as Thomas regained his balance and threw his burden to the ground. The jerk grabbed at my arm, but I stomped on his toes and pushed him away.

"Bryce? Honey? Can you hear me?" I cupped my fiancé's face lightly. Thomas snatched a handful of my hair and yanked.

"You're going to pay for that," he snarled. I twisted in his hold and kicked at him.

"Oh, leave off!" I told him, slapping at his arm and digging my nails into his skin. "And let go of my hair, you stupid ape!"

"Now, Miss Watson," Morrissey soothed. "Try to be reasonable here. Thomas does have a gun."

"Like I'll go anywhere without Bryce," I retorted, fighting wildly against Thomas's hold. "Call off your brute if you want me to be reasonable."

"Thomas, enough. Let the young lady go."

Thomas gave my head a sharp, painful heave before backing away. I crawled over to Bryce. His eyelids fluttered and I let out a sigh of relief. "Bryce, can you hear me?"

He groaned and turned his head, and I huffed at him. Not even a tiny knot on the side of his head. Nor the makings of a bruise. I managed to do worse cleaning my shower stall. Patting him lightly on the cheek, I said, "Bryce, wake up."

He groaned again and cracked an eye at me. "Bryce, you're milking it," I told him and gave a playful slap on his jaw. He grimaced and pulled himself upright, holding his head.

"Why are you still here? I gave you a clear escape route, and you're still here. I swear, Lily…"

I shrugged, "You needed saving."

"You should have run when you had the chance."

A throat cleared behind us. "Mr. King, Miss Watson, if you please—"

We both ignored him. I put my hands on my hips and glared at Bryce. "And what would you have done? Take on both of them? Idiot over there has a gun if you haven't noticed, and I am not getting married to a man with holes in him."

"*I* would have waited for the cavalry," he said calmly. "You're the one who would have gotten herself shot. Just what do you think you would have done, huh?"

"Mr. King…Miss Watson…"

"What cavalry?" I demanded. "No one knows we're out here with these idiots."

"If you please…" Morrissey tried again. Thomas locked his fingers around my elbow. I jerked away and glared at my future husband.

Bryce stood face to face with me, getting angrier by the second. "I'm not responsible for this, if that's what you're getting at."

I thumped him in the chest. "I'm not saying that you are. But since you brought it up, you must have done something to get your guilty conscience all worked up. Tell me what it is."

"Or what?" Bryce demanded, tilting his head down for effect, making me very aware of the fact that he was several inches taller than me. Now, that was a cheap shot.

Thomas looked to his employer for guidance. Morrissey stepped closer. "If you two will—"

"Shut up!" Bryce and I said at him together. I added, "We're having a lover's spat, if you don't mind."

"This is not a lover's spat," Bryce corrected. "You were being held hostage, and I'm upset that you didn't run when the opportunity presented itself. What would a little woman like you have done? Take on two grown men at the same time?"

"It wouldn't be the first time," I declared hotly.

Thomas waved his gun in our view. "Hey! I have a gun!"

I rounded on him. "Do you *mind*?! And didn't I tell you that if I ever saw you again, I'd shove a pry bar into your skull?"

Bryce turned me by my shoulder. "What do you mean 'again'? Do you know him?"

"Meet Fireman Thomas," I presented the gun-flashing fool in a haughty tone. "Bently's idea of a practical joke, I'm sure."

Benjamin Morrissey watched us spar with the funniest look on his face. "Are you two always like this?"

"Actually, yes," Bryce said and smiled lovingly at me. "Isn't she the greatest?"

"Don't you dare try to sweet-talk me, Mr. King," I said to him, with a smile of my own, and then whispered, "Save it for later."

"Later, it is. Now tell me how you know Thomas

Hall."

I hitched a shoulder, rolled my eyes in disgust, and snatched my water bottle off the end table. "He's been stalking me."

~~~~~

Bryce closed his eyes. He couldn't believe her. Here she was, a gun pointed at her, and she was shrugging off the whole ordeal as nothing special. She even had the nerve to pick a fight with him. God, he loved her!

"I beg your pardon?"

Lily giggled as she took a sip, spitting water down the front of her shirt. "You know, I used to hate it when you said that."

"Explain the stalking," he demanded. Thomas glanced at Morrissey one last time, puffed out a breath of frustration and slumped against the wall, the handgun hanging by his side. Lily watched him, her eyes taking in every movement. He knew that look. He knew it well. What was she planning?

Lily pointed her bottle at Thomas. "I met him through Bently, who has a lot of explaining to do. I thought Bently had better taste in friends. He's been trying to get me to go out with him for a month now. However, I know for a fact that you are not a fireman."

The gun rose in the air. "What gave it away?" Thomas asked sarcastically.

"Your hands," lily answered, ignoring the weapon. "Soft as a baby's bottom. I'm surprised that pea-shooter isn't giving you a blister."

Morrissey actually snorted a laugh, covering it up with a cough. "Maybe now we can get down to business," he said, directing a stern look at each of them.

Bryce turned to him, stuffing his hands in his pants pockets. "What do you want? Watson won his case. And when I get the evidence of your involvement, there will be nothing you can ever do to me. You murdered a man—"

Morrissey stopped him there, "On the contrary, Nicolas Garcia wasn't murdered. He killed himself."

"What?" Lily asked, startled.

"Yes, Miss Watson, your ex-husband really did kill himself," Morrissey nodded. "I, nor any of my associates, had anything to do with it. His death was a convenient turn of events. Unfortunately the evidence on that matter was, shall we say, never reported."

"Nick drowned in the middle of a lake," Lily said. "He didn't get there by himself."

"Mr. Garcia's blood results contained a large amount of sedatives..."

Bryce held up his hand, "Wait. Nick didn't swallow sleeping pills and then decide to go for a boat ride."

"And alcohol," Morrissey added. "A tragedy, really, but not my fault. I'm still confused on how he managed to get his boat back to dock."

Lily stared at the older man. "Your wife died that way, didn't she?"

Cold composure masked the real emotions beneath Morrissey's hooded eyes. Bryce felt the temperature in the room drop by several degrees. Thomas shifted uneasily in the corner, and everyone noticed the movement. He cringed as three sets of eyes settled on him. A faint tint of shame rose on the man's neck.

"Thomas?" Bryce inquired with a raised eyebrow. "Care to share something?"

Thomas' chin lifted violently in the air. "I don't know what you're talking about."

"Oh, I think you do," Bryce said in a low tone. "Did you kill Nick Garcia, Thomas?"

Thomas ignored the question and advanced to the center of the room, so that Bryce, Lily, and Morrissey were in his sights. The barrel of the gun drew level with the older man's chest. "Charlotte was an angel," he snarled at his employer. "And you killed her. She did everything for you, and you just shoved her aside without any concern for her feelings. All she wanted from you was some attention. Just some goddamn attention."

Morrissey paled.

The gun swiveled to Bryce. "And you," Thomas continued, "she came to you for comfort - comfort that she should have asked me for. And what did you do? You turned away from her as well. Charlotte was a fragile flower, a beautiful lady that needed someone to love her the way she deserved. Neither of you saw that in her. Neither of you cared."

Lily tilted her head to the side. "But you cared, didn't you, Thomas?"

The weapon in his hands shook. "Yes, I cared. I loved her. And she didn't want me. She wanted you," he said, speaking to Morrissey, "and you," he said to Bryce.

"Never me, but I was there. I was always there. I found her, do you remember that? It was me that found her lying in her bathtub, cold and lifeless."

Bryce watched as Lily put the water bottle down and stepped closer to Thomas. He shook his head at her. Don't do anything stupid, he pleaded silently.

"Thomas, did you kill Nick?" she asked softly.

"Nick," Thomas snorted. "Another man who Charlotte went to for love. Oh yes, he cared. He cared so much that he was going to take her away from me. But I got rid of him. He never saw her again."

Lily looked at Morrissey, "I thought your wife died a few years ago. Nick was killed only last month."

"That's correct," Morrissey said, eyeing Thomas with new insight.

"How long have you been divorced?" Bryce asked Lily.

"Three years," she said. "Does that have anything to do with Charlotte's death?"

Thomas sneered at all of them. "I told him to stay away from Charlotte. I told him that she would never fall for a married man. But she did, and after she died, he disappeared. It took me a long time to find him, and find a way to make him pay. To make all of you pay."

Okay, Lily knew that Nick cheated on her, but Bryce didn't want to think she'd ever have to face the evidence of it. He glanced at her. White lines formed around her mouth, and those lovely, spunky blue eyes were alight with a flickering inferno. She inched forward, balling her fists, and Thomas swung to face her. She halted, dark, dangerous shadows forming under her eyes. "And then

I met you," Thomas said. "'Get close to the family,' Ben told me. 'See if we can use them to our advantage', but I met you. Garcia's ex-wife. And what do you know? You look just like Charlotte. My Charlotte."

"I do?" she asked, blinking at him, and then turned to Bryce. "Do I?"

"Now that you mention it," Morrissey began. Bryce nodded, seeing the resemblance. The eyes were different, and Charlotte was a good half foot taller, but yes, the two women could have been sisters, or closely related.

Thomas' voice cracked. "And I thought I found my Charlie girl again. But did you want me either? No! You were in love with this asshole. I should have made you mine, should have taken what I wanted anyway. But that P.I. your fiancé hired found me, and I didn't get the opportunity. Now, I do," he shrugged and laughed shrilly, "now you get to pay for Charlotte's death, too. You all do."

"How do you plan to do that?" Lily wanted to know as she took another step closer to him.

Thomas nodded like a lunatic, his eyes glittering bizarrely. "Oh, yes. I set it all up. I introduced Vivian to you, Benjamin, and I made sure she struck a deal with Mr. King here."

Bryce swallowed. He'd known Vivian for years. "Does Vivian know any of this?"

"That stupid chit? She doesn't have a clue," Thomas sneered. "Once Watson Construction became the property of King Enterprises, I doped up Nick with sleeping pills and dumped him into the lake. Everything else fell into place, just like I planned."

"And now, Thomas?" Bryce asked, shifting to the side so that Lily was no longer in the madman's sight. "What are your plans now?"

Thomas gave a sinister chuckle. "Oh, I'm going to shoot you in the head, while your woman watches. And then I'm going to kill Mr. Morrissey, and then take my time with the lovely Miss Watson. But she will die, too; don't worry about that. She will die, too. And then Charlotte and I will be together again soon. We'll be together again."

Bryce hoped that Thomas had thought this plan thorough for his own sake. In no known universe would Lily just stand by and watch the crazy bastard kill any of them. Not Lily Watson. She had a wedding to plan and a baby to care for. No, Lily Watson wasn't dying today. Already, she was scowling at the man and digging her nails into her palms, daring him to make a single move.

Lord, he hoped she appreciated the bullet he was about to take for her.

~~~~~

Bryce shook his head at me one more time. I clenched my teeth. I wasn't just going to stand there and be target practice for this crazy moron. Morrissey's pale face and shocked stillness told me that he wasn't about to do anything to help us. And Bryce...

I sighed.

Handling overbearing men was second nature to me. I worked in construction, for God's sake! If he thought he was going to save me, he had another thing coming. I'd never be able to look the man in the eye.

Bryce edged further away, drawing Thomas' attention. I cast him a "Stop helping!" look and scanned the room for something to smash against Baby Hands' ugly head. Suddenly Bryce dove at Thomas, scaring the life out of me. A deafening bang echoed in the room. I picked up the first large object within reach, a heavy iron candlestick, and clonked Thomas just behind his right ear.

Both men went tumbling to the floor. Morrissey didn't move at all...he just stood there, and I huffed at all of them.

"Bryce, are you shot?" I asked, tugging Thomas to the side and off of the man I loved. "You better not be shot. I'm not spending my wedding day in the hospital with you, dang it. I mean it, Bryce King! If you're shot, I'm taking three months to plan the biggest wedding you can afford. No three-day-waiting-period crap this time...Bryce?"

A humorous chuckle reverberated up from the woven rug. "Remind me to get rid of every candlestick in the house. You're a dangerous woman, Lily Watson."

I grinned down at him. His russet hair lay over his forehead, and a glimmer of fear still shone in his eyes, but he was safe. No extra holes. That was a good thing. "Well, if you had died, I'd have to revive you just to smack you a good one. What on earth were you doing? I'm trying to keep you alive, and you go and tackle the man with the gun. Are you demented?"

"Say 'Thank you, Bryce'," he said, rising to his feet,

giving Thomas a good kick in the ribs, just in case. "Say, 'I love you, and you are the bravest man on the planet.' Say it, or the wedding's off."

I shook my head. "'I love you'," I quoted, "but the rest of that will not pass my lips."

He kicked the gun out of Thomas' unconscious hand, and drew me up to his chest. "I'll pass something through your lips," he murmured and kissed me soundly and rightfully. Morrissey blinked once before he ran out of the door. Bryce sighed.

"The police will get him later, I suppose."

"Damn straight they will," I said and stole me another kiss. I moaned against his mouth when my head stopped spinning, "Now, what's this about you hiring a private investigator to keep an eye on me?"

Just in case you were wondering...

Thomas Hall was arrested and convicted of three counts of attempted murder, one count of premeditated murder – as a result of Nick's exhumed body and new autopsy – and a long list of other crimes that boggled my mind. Benjamin Morrissey was charged with a few felonies as well, and both spent a good amount of time in tiny, cement block rooms. Thomas earned a few calluses the hard way. And not all of them were on his hands.

The following Saturday, Bryce hired out the entire golf course at his country club. We were married on the first green, and spent the rest of the day playing golf with everyone we knew. Lisa's boys enjoyed the game, running up and down the fairways without restraint, and Bryce won by a birdie.

I never did forgive Bryce for trying to save me, but I thought up creative measures for his penance, which he only happily agreed to.

And eight months later, I gave birth to a beautiful baby girl, who we named Jacqueline, after his mother, and Momma and Daddy spoiled her rotten.

Bryce got the final word in when he signed Daisy as Jackie's middle name, and didn't tell me about it until I received the official birth certificate in the mail a few weeks later. He's still paying for that stunt.

Oh, and I designed a house for Lisa and her family that she loved, adding one of those electronic chef programs that walk her through the steps of recipes exactly the way they should be prepared, via a monitor inlaid in her king-sized kitchen island. Bryce and I have dinner over there once a week now...without complaint.

Jackie grew up to be beautiful and smart and active and so completely normal that at the age of fifteen, she beat Bri's record for most groundings in a single month. She had some help, of course. Her twin, baby brothers caused a lot of trouble for her. Bryce still coped with the fact that all his children were perfectly normal in every way, except for a few traumatic moments when they walked in on me and Bryce, um...talking.

Hey! There was nothing wrong with having a "conversation" on the kitchen counter in the middle of a Sunday. Nothing wrong with that at all.

Heather McGhee lives in central Arkansas, sharing her life and days with her loving, playful husband, her two equally-playful children, a cat which only tolerates her, and the swarms of mosquitoes that make the summer nights interesting. As a child, writing was her dream, but as an adult, writing has become her obsession, resulting in unusual side-effects, such as selective-hearing and discriminatory blindness to the chaos around her.

My Own Worst Nightmare is her second book, though not the last. As an avid participant on Wattpad.com (another fixation), she is constantly uploading new chapters to her romances, chatting with e-fans, and devouring the imaginative tales of other writers.

If she could have anything in the world, those things would be an extra hour in the day and an extra brain in her head, to use exclusively for storing all the ideas she keeps forgetting.